To: Ms. Karen

B-More
Loyal
30 Years Before Dishonor

From: Christph White
& White
Pamela & Kim
& Jr

Chris White 12/5/22

Order via email: Urbansoup2020@gmail.com

ISBN:-13: 978-1523409310
ISBN-10: 1523409312

Cover Design: Eric Horace
BlazinGraphxx

DEDICATION

Dedicated to: Mrs. Pamela White AKA Super Mom!!
Ma I hope and pray that you're found to be in the very best of
health and spirits. Keep God first in everything that you do.

In the name of Jesus Christ my Lord and Savior... Amen.!!

I would like to introduce my best friend and soulmate to the
world. I would like to acknowledge the most special and sacred
jewel ever known to a man. I'm saying that I've never in all of my
life met a true and best friend such as this great woman right here.
I mean she's built better than any kind of Ford Motor car or truck
that they have ever made. It's like God just dropped her right out
of Heaven to me. She's real and don't run from me and hide, or
give up and turn her back on me when things get bad and prison
comes into out mist. A lot of people I know gave up on me and
moved on without me when things got bad for me, but this great
woman ran to my aide and loved me through it all. Love became a
great action word for her, because this woman made it her business
to put me first in everything. She drives 12 or 13 hours to visit and
be with me faithfully. We've built a real life and real bond. I
thank God for blessing me with the most precious gift ever. She's
been putting in work all around typing books, editing books, and
handling whatever had to be done to create it and got it done. She
had never ever been a procrastinator or nothing close to it. She is
the truth... Thank you very much Chandra Lee White.

I dedicate this book to my Lord and Savior Jesus Christ for

saving my life and allowing me to use my talents that I never really knew existed. Also, this book is dedicated to my #1 Super Mom, Mrs. Pamela White, who allowed me to be myself and love me no matter what I did, who stuck with me even while this storm was going on. I just wanted to tell my Mom that we finally made it. Here's the book that the Lord blessed my mind to write for you and the rest of this world. This is a very good story to read; this book was written and created by the Spirit of God. I was just a vessel that God decided to use, and I yielded and allowed God to have His way with me.

People, everyone has a story, if you will allow Jesus Christ to guide you and use you, anyone can do this. Accept Jesus Christ and watch your life change for the better. You must truly believe in yourself and in your heart that everything that God speaks, He will do it and you will be blessed and highly favored. I love you Super Mom!!!

Rest in peace all of my people and May God keep you. To my loving grandma: Mrs. Laura Humphrey. Man grandma it's been a very long time now and I still keep you safe in my heart. How can I ever forget you? (Well that answer is never, you feel me). I think of you more then you will ever know. You were one of my best friends you know that right? If you did not, then I'm telling you that you were. I know that you are resting in peace and I hope and pray that you like this master piece that God has allowed me to put together. It's such a great blessing to be able to love and honor you still to this very day. I remember so clearly the day that you looked across the way and asked me what I was over there doing, and you know that I was over there mixing up like crazy. You had even scared me a lil bit that night too. Well I just wanted to let you know that I still love you and keep you in my heart and I carry you everywhere I go too.
Rest in Peace Grandma......

Hey Daddy, I know that you are wondering about me right now. I'm doing fine, you feel me just trying to work hard like I always be doing, but this time God is in full control of my life. I sometimes wonder just how my life would have turned out if you would have never left us. Maybe, just maybe I would not be in prison, but I can't even cry over any spilled milk, I do miss you as well, I just wish that we could have done better. Who knows maybe you are saved and I'll get another chance to see you in Heaven? I hope that you got saved Dad. You know that nobody but mommy really believed in me and my dreams right. Well, it's not just a dream no more, I have made it into a reality. My book is on it's way up there to you in heaven if that's where you are at, Oh, yea I forgot to tell you I have one out already. It is called "A Taste of Urban Soup for the People's Soul". I do want you to read it and see that your first born was really worth the time and energy that you and mommy put into creating me along with the help of God, allowing you to have a chance to create children. Well my friend I hope you are doing well and keep my name before God while you're resting in peace up there. Watch over me too. I love you.

Rest in Peace Daddy......

ACKNOWLEDGMENTS

What's up, lil homie? I know that you were here and I do love you and I miss you (Phylicia Barnes). I'm with you in spirit and I want you to know that everyone loves you and misses you like crazy. I prayed for you so many nights, hoping that it wasn't going to ever come down to this, but God saw something that we all couldn't, you feel me. Man you made the news a lot of times, everyone was looking for you and I want you to know that you are still very important to everyone. When I saw you're pretty little face flash across that TV. Screen, I thought about my little girl as well. That could have very well been anyone's little girl out there missing like that. God will get whoever did that to you. He see's everything and everyone. I just hope that you can read this book in the spirit. I pray that your mother and father are found to be doing well; I also, want you to keep a good watch over me too. You are a very special angel; you do know that right? I have never forgotten you even when things had come to a close, I still kept you alive in my heart and around the world as each and every book go around to different parts of the world people will remember your name. Talk about you like you are still around and guess what little homie? You are to me... Well I will not hold you long just wanted to keep you alive when all of the millions of people read this joint they will see your name and know that you was a somebody, I love you little home girl.

I would also like to acknowledge my 3 children as well, I love all 3 of you guys and I'm sorry that this happened to me but I'll be back to get you guys too. I love you (Christopher White Jr. 3rd, aka Scoop, Christian White, aka Yonk Yonk and last but not least, Shatiera White aka my little princess). I just want you all to know that you all 5 people are the most important people in my life. I'll be home to you all soon!! Also, to all of my homies that read my first print when the words were so little that you couldn't even read it, but kept me going and made me keep on pushing it and never gave up on me.

For the ones who kept on asking me where was the rest

of it at, you all helped me to know that I really had something that was real and positive for once in my life. I thank all of you, also shout out to Brother Brown for allowing the Holy Spirit to move on him and search my heart to see that I was who I came to him as, and for helping me to get back under that powerful order of God's operation. The same operation that Adam fell from under, I'm now back under it and God is back in full control of my life again.

Thank you Brother Brown for the amazing life changing Bible course that you have been sharing with so many brothers and changing lives daily with God in control of all that you say and do for us brothers. Thank you for helping me bring my project into the full manifestation from the Super Natural powers of God himself... Shout out to your book publishing company as well. (Divine Royalty Publishing Company), also people check out his books that are changing lives all over the world, Go to his site www.divineroyaltypublishingcompany.com.

His books are powerful. Shout out to my partner Solo from Chi-town, man you are one heck of a dude and you keep me grounded and rooted. You came through in the clutch a few times when I was steady burning them type writer ribbons up, you had one or 2 for me every time so you know that I could never ever forget about you. everything counts, to my homie for life

Keon Williams from east Baltimore, man you really were a part of this B-More loyal movement for real you even took time to dissect every page and knew it by heart and wrote down the stuff that I had missed and helped me to take out the things that did not belong, thank you for doing that for me, to my main man Lavert Finny from Akron Ohio, you were here with me when the story first hit the paper and we was doing this together. You still my man and I'll be back to get you okay much love my nigga. Shout to my big sister (Check), you kept me going to all of your many prayers, and your emails helped too. Thanks you Check, shout out to everyone who gave that extra push that we all need at times to know that we are on the path. There are so many names I really don't want to forget anyone so shout out to everyone!!

CHAPTER 1

In the beginning it was me, my mother, and my 2 sisters. Everything kicked off in 1989. When I was growing up it was all bad, until one day my dude Apple Sider came to holla at me. Apple said, "Black I'm tired of seeing you looking and dressing like that, you know that I got that work for you black 60/40".

My mother had always told me to stay the heck away from the drug game, so I always said in response was "I'm good Apple". I was just lying, knowing dag on well that I really needed a big break in my life. My shoes had big holes in them, running over, leaning to the side, so my shoes were what we all would call being on the half. My sisters were on the half right along with me. Everyone was always on us hard, cracking their little funny jokes. This was going on in school and just about any and everywhere else we went. Black always had that killer hustle inside of him. His mother was a good hustler so that torch was passed down to him through his bloodline. Every day after school Black went down to the Stop Shop, and Save Super Market, to bag and carry different people's bags for all kinds of small change and sometimes depending on how far Black had to go before he would reach the person's car or house he would earn dollars. Black had started growing real tired of just carrying bags and making small change, so one day he went to have a sit down with his mother Penny about the street life and selling drugs. Penny knew just about everything that there was to know about them mean streets of Baltimore City. She ran the streets every day and every night. Penny explained to Black everything that there was to know about the street life. She schooled him on the rules to being a street hustler, the most important #1 rule and code of the streets was that Black had to become a man and always stand, plus be able to always hold his own. The code of the streets is always, if you every get locked up out there hustling, selling drugs, or doing whatever it is that you think that you want to do out there in those streets you can't every tell on anyone, be a man do your time.

Penny then asked Black, "So are you really ready for what's out there in that street life?"

Black was looking into his mother's eyes with tears inside his that he wouldn't allow to fall.

Black said, "I better be ready for this street life, because the truth be told I'm really tired of starving some nights, not having new shoes and clothes, and everyone cracking their little jokes on us, I see now, Ma that I have to go out and make it happen for myself, because it sure don't seem like it's going to just fall out of the sky for me, so yea Ma I'm really ready for that so-called street life".

That night Black had made up his mind that it was now or never. Black and his 2 sisters Lisa and Chrissy all slept in the same bedroom for many years together. That night it was something that was very different, because Black was crying to himself and both of his sisters couldn't seem to understand why in the world their big brother was crying. Chrissy and Lisa had both got out of their bunk beds and came to comfort their brother, but to their surprise Black was crying, no doubt about it, but they were all tears of joy, Black knew what was up ahead of him was soon to be his future. He knew that once morning came, it would be the end of all of his struggling days. Black sat down and he told his 2 sisters all about his run in with the dude Apple Sider, and also his talk with their mother Penny and how she put him on point and her schooling him to the street life. He also, told them how he was just so tired of not having and seeing them doing badly, Black knew what his next move was going to be, and his mind was set on him hitting the block bright and early in the morning. Black didn't know anything about the street life or the drug game, but he was very strong and eager to learn and come up out of the bottomless pit. Every morning, Penny would be yelling at the top of her lungs for her 3 children to get their butt's up and go wash up, brush their teeth, eat and get ready for school. To Penny's surprise, when she came into the children's room Black wasn't nowhere to be found. Chrissy and Lisa got up, got themselves ready, but it really puzzled Penny that Black wasn't nowhere to be found in the house.

Penny asked her daughters, "Where is ya'll brother at?", They both looked at each other and said at the same time "Ma we haven't seen him, he was in here with us last night right before we all went to sleep".

Penny said, "That dag on boy is really going to make me hurt his butt". Once everyone had gone to sleep, Black had got up and left the house way earlier than usual, so that he could catch up with his dude Apple Sider, right before he opened up his shop. Black came walking down the street calling out to Apple Sider.

Black said "Yo Apple, what's up?"

Apple Sider heard someone calling out to him and when he turned around to see who was calling him, he saw that it was Black.

Apple answered "Oh what's up Black, you sure are out here mighty early in the morning aren't you? What's the deal?" Black looked into Apple's eyes and said "Yo, I'm ready to get this money", Apple looked at him and smiled for a minute. Apple said "I knew that you had that killer hustler mentality in you. You know something Black?"

Black said "What Apple?"

Apple replied, "I've been waiting for your arrival for a few months now". From that day forth Black never ever looked back, Black started getting money, slinging that coke 60/40, left and right.

Black was going hard in the paint, hand to hand, getting his shine on hard. While hustling Black's only lines that he would be quoting to people is that: I got them big blues right here, meaning that he had tall glass vials of coke cocaine, fish scale to the top." Big blues is what all of the junkies wanted, the people who used the drugs that Black had, He had what they wanted, and he had that good good. One day while on the block, Apple Sider had told Black that before he knew it that them 60/40 packs would have him sitting fat in a minute.

Apple also told Black to make sure that he put some money up for them rainy days.

Apple said "Black rainy days are on the way, it is for real my nigga be ready for them."

Apple was telling Black to be prepared for them when they did come. Black heard it all, but he didn't take heed or listen to Apple Sider. Apple was trying to teach him about rainy days, but Black didn't listen to him Black was killing the game. He had made like $100,000.00 dollars in 2 months. Black had started shopping, buying new shoes, clothes, and he was keeping himself well groomed, plus taking care of his family.

Black had even gone as far as buying himself a new car. It was an "88" Nissan Maxima that he copped from down V.A., everyone went down V.A. to buy their cars, because as long as you had the money you could get anything that you wanted to get, any kind of cars you wanted and all you needed was the cash and whoever name you wanted to car titles to be in, it was done. Black was shining, getting plenty of girls and starting to just spend his money all crazy. He started slacking on the block, getting too relaxed, comfortable, chilling, parting and one day Black went back to his money stash and only had $250.00 dollars cash left to his name.

He had a lot of brand new clothes, shoes, girls, and a car, Black was never taught how to manage his money right and right now he was learning a valuable lesson. He sat down and thought really hard for just a quick minute, and then it all hit him like a ton of bricks, it all started to make perfect sense to him. He now finally got what Apple Sider was trying to teach him about them rainy days. From that day forth Black had made up his mind that he was going to buckle back down again and get his money back right again, but what Black really didn't know was that when it rains it pours down like crazy. He went to see Apple Sider so that he could get back on again with the 60/40 packs, but Apple Sider was now off, meaning that he was chilling at the time that Black really needed to get some more packs from him. Now Black was furious not knowing what else or who else it was that he could get some work from. So, Black had just gone on home that day. He kept on counting that same $250 dollars over and over again, but then an idea had popped into his mind as he thought of his other dude who was getting money real heavy on the mean streets of B-more.

His name is T-Mac, He is the man for real. He had all kinds of cars, jewelry, girls and he is known for doing it really big. So, Black saw T-Mac driving by the next day and flagged him down and explained his situation. He told T-Mac what was up and what he was trying to do, but the problem that Black had was that T-Mac didn't deal in any small nickel and dime or small weight. Black climbed up inside of T-Mac's Bronco truck and they drove around for a little while.

Black explained his self, while T-Mac contemplated if he was going to allow Black to get some money with him or not. T-Mac finally told Black that he would help him to get back on his feet and get some real money again, but that he had to keep on copping his work from him only. Black shook T-Mac's hand to seal their deal.

T-Mac said, "Yo, give me the $200 dollars you have and I'll sell you a quarter ounce of coke". Black reached inside of his pocket and gave T-Mac the $200 dollars which had left him 50 dollars to his name, and then he had to go to the vail store and buy 2 packs of vails which cost him $30. Black now had just 20 dollars left.

Black was thinking out loud and said to himself "If only I would have listened to Apple Sider about these rainy days, I would not be at this point right now. I can't cry over spilled milk now because setbacks like this comes with the game". At least that's what Black kept on telling himself. Black went on home that night and his mother Penny was very happy for her son. His 2 sisters were even happier that their big brother was doing his thing, at lease that is how a lot of the things had appeared to everyone who was just looking in from the outside. Black only had 20 dollars left from the 250 that he had left from his stash and Chrissy and Lisa just came and took the last 20 that he had left. They needed 10 dollars for their school lunch for the week and just from Black's outer appearance he couldn't say no to his 2 sisters. As the weeks passed by Black grew smarter and smarter.

He started stacking his money fast and hard this time around. Black would take baths and showers, change his under clothes and socks, but he would always put the same clothes right back on. One day while he was in grind mode, Black had met this girl named Dia. Dia was so pretty, sexy, and bad. Everyone in the hood wanted to holla at Dia, but it was just something about Black's swagger that just made Dia melt inside. Black always loved to listen to slow music and he would always carry his small tape recorder with him. His favorite song was by the group Color Me Bad; I want to sex you up. Little did Black know, but that was Dia's favorite song as well. Dia use to always chase after Black trying to take his tape recorder from him, so that she could hear her favorite song that he was rocking. Black and Dia had started to grow to be mad cool as the weeks passed them by. Black was now back focused, still in grind mode, still getting that money, but stacking it all this time around. Dia liked Black so much that one day she had surprised him, she walked up to him and planted the most softest and sweetest kiss ever on Black's lips, after that kiss, Black was in love with Dia.

They exchanged numbers and use to stay up all hours of the night just talking on the phone and listening to each other just breathe. Black and Dia had grown to be inseparable. One day Black had asked Dia to make their relationship official and be his girlfriend, and he told her that this is what he wanted from her. I need your love and loyalty more than anything else in the world. Black had other lil friends that he had met, but it was never anything serious like he was about Dia. She told Black that she would be the one for him and that she would love him and stay loyal to him. Word was spreading around B-More that Black was involved with a new girl named Dia. Dia was way more than a dime piece and all of the other girls had started to wonder what was up with Black if Dia was so in love with him.

Black went from that quarter ounce to a half, from a half to a whole ounce, then he went to 2 ounces, from 2-4 ½, from 4 ½ to 9 ounces, from 9 to 18 and then before Black knew it or even realized it he had started coping 2 kilos of coke at a time. Black kept his word to T-Mac and he was still copping from him. Black was all the way back on his feet now. Black had got his own little apartment; Black took care of everyone that he loved. His girl Dia, mother and sister's was all that he really had. Black had started switching cars and he was all the way back on top of the world again. But, this time around he was going to be for real about his paper. Black is now officially a boss. Everything that Black has done was all coming from him getting money from up where he grew up on Whitelock St. and Lakeview Ave. Black knew other dudes that he had grew up with, who also was getting a lot of money, but Black was set apart from all of the rest.

He was getting his own money and other dudes were also doing them. Black didn't have any partners or crews; he was a one-man army. Chuck was a go getter as well, he had a lot of goons on his payroll and his team was taking down big, but nobody could every count Black's money. Black was never ever pressed or concerned about what everyone else was taking in. Black didn't have any time to worry about nothing else; Sampson was another dude that was getting a lot of money from up on Whitelock Street. He was getting major paper from way back in the days, like the early 80's so it was too hard to ever count his money as well. Sampson is a millionaire easy, and nobody up on Whitelock Street has ever been on his level. Toney is a nerd, he's what you would call a school boy; he doesn't have a hustling bone in his body. He doesn't know anything at all about the street life, but Sampson went on ahead and took Tony in and he's forgotten all about his school work. He just came straight off of the steps getting money with Sampson. Ricky, Yummy, Ty-Ty, Terrell, and Calvin are all running with Chuck and they were all getting a lot of paper. They all have big cars and are doing their thing. Every last one of Chuck's goons are eating good, they all had nice girls. Black has girls' is an understatement. Black has too many girls but he always tried to do his very best to respect Dia, who is his main girl. Sampson has a nice fleet of girls as well, but Sampson's problem is that he always seems to fall in love with every girl that he meets. Everyone is from up on Whitelock and everyone is getting and seeing a nice piece of money from this hood.

As the years keep on passing by, Black somehow ends up befriending Tony and they hook up together and they branch off to a whole other area. Black was well known from all over, Black and Tony started running a shop in another part of Baltimore City. One day Black had went to talk to his man

even know who's who out in them streets, but in due time everything and everyone must reveal itself. That's the law of nature in that order. Ecclesiastes (3): God said it's a time for everything. As the weeks kept passing by Dia's belly kept growing and she was indeed pregnant by Black. She was at the market one day and she ran into Black's sister Chrissy, who was very happy to see Dia. Chrissy would always say this same thing to Dia every time they saw each other.

Chrissy said, "Girl I haven't' seen you in a month of Sunday's, where have you been at "Oh, I know now, you need to keep them legs closed and stay out of that dag on bed, you and my brother. Look at you all big and stuff, carrying my niece or nephew. I'm so happy for ya'll."

Now, Chrissy wasn't bad looking either, but whenever any girl came into Dia's presence bells went off, Chrissy is 5'10, 155lbs, nice breast, brown skin, she's cute, favors Black a lot, but she's a girl. She's got a phat booty, big legs, and she wears a size 8 in shoes, so her feet are small, but Dia's feet are size 3 ½ or 4. Dia and Chrissy did their food shopping together. As they were going from one isle to the next, Dia's mind was racing.

Dia asked Chrissy, "How is Mrs. Penny doing? Because she hadn't seen her in a while."

Chrissy answered, "That Penny was cooling and just wondering how Black was doing."

CHAPTER 3

Penny hasn't seen her son that much here lately, maybe in traffic every now and then. Penny was really starting to miss her son. It seemed like the only time that she ever got to see him was when he was either bringing her some money or ripping and running the mean hardcore streets of Baltimore city. Penny still had a few things jumping out in the streets too. She's still the master mind and the one who blessed her son Black and gave him the green light, the game so that he could go out and become the man and hustler that he is right now. Black was always very thankful for his mother Penny.

She taught him everything that he needed to know, to make it. Black's father is no show in all of his children's lives. Black's father name is Big Clifford aka Big Cliff, but Black has always hated his father with a passion. His father is 6'2 190 lbs., brown skin with 3 golds in his mouth, 2 up top and 1 at the very bottom of his mouth. It's kind of strange that Black has 5 up top and 1 at the bottom like his father. Big Cliff never ever spend no real time with his children nor had he ever brought his children anything, but a serious void in their lives and in their hearts. Big Cliff is the reason why Black had to start hitting the streets of B-More so hard, getting all of that dope money, because he had to grow up and become a man at such a very young age, with no father figure.

Black had vowed to never ever abandon none of his children once they were born. His father Big Cliff left a broken family shattered into so many pieces that could never ever again be put back together again.

Big Cliff wasn't anything in Black's eyes; it was really bad blood between him and his father. Black just really could never understand how a man could just up and leave his children that way that his so-called father did this. Big Cliff made Black grow up without him, no father figure and the sad part of this is Black's father was able to be a dad to them. Black's father wasn't in jail or anything, but it's amazing at how strong Penny has been for her children. She's an extra. Supermom as Black calls her.

Penny is mom and dad all wrapped into one person. Big Cliff didn't have an alibi as to why he wasn't a father to his 3 children by Penny. He left Penny to struggle on welfare and whatever money she made on them streets of B-More. Right after Chrissy and Dia parted ways to get to their respective houses, and Chrissy was just pulling up and parking her car which she had just bought. She had a new Honda accord. Chrissy has just parked her car when her drunken sister Lisa was pulling up right behind her, driving like a bat out of hell. Lisa was a little crazy at times, she was indeed drunk. She is dark skinned, 5'8 and 190lbs, brown eyes; she's cute, looks like Black as well. Lisa is kind of on the chubby side, big titties and super phat butt, her titties are a size 44dd's and she could most definitely knock a dude out with those big jugs.

Lisa loves that bottle to death; all she wants to do is drink 24/7 a day. She drinks for no reason, and she always stirs up a whole lot of trouble all of the time. Black never liked to give Lisa no kind of money because all she would do is spend it all on her beer, but Lisa wasn't drinking she was cool as a fan. Black hated seeing his sister Lisa in a drunken state. She would get drunk and cuss any and every one out. Lisa didn't care who you were, she would cuss you out so bad, and be ready to fight you. After, Chrissy got all of the bags out of the trunk of the car, she went in the house and put all of the food away, then she called Dia up to make sure that she made it back in the house safely.

Dia's phone rang like 6 times before she heard her big brother's voice come to life.

Black answered the phone, "What it do"? Chrissy was so happy to hear Black's voice since she had not heard anything from him in a little while.

Chrissy repeated it right back to him "what it do then Big Head?"

Black instantly busted out laughing at her for trying to imitate the way that he talked. All of the women that Black loved and cared about all loved just how smooth Black was when he did anything, even when talking to them.

Chrissy spoke first and said "what's up big bro?'

Black just smiled at her through the phone and said, "You know me sis, just out here getting this paper and trying to keep it coming in."

Chrissy said, "That's what's up, I was calling to see if Dia got back from the market safely?"

Black said, "Yea, she is in the kitchen right now putting the food away."

Chrissy replied, "Black I saw her tummy too, that girl pregnant carrying my lil niece or nephew. Black how come you didn't you tell me that you had a lil shorty on the way?"

After Chrissy asked Black that question concerning his lil shorty, it brought back a flood gate of old memories about their no good, lying half a man father Big Cliff. Black's mind had drifted off back to when he was a lil shorty, and they were living on Lexington St. and the house had an upstairs and a down stairs bathroom, living room, dining room and kitchen, plus a nice size basement. One day, when Black was little he came down the back steps of the house so that he could use the down stairs bathroom to take a poop, and low and behold, Black found his father sitting on the toilet with a needle in his arm. Seeing this for the very first time in his life he was scared to death, and Black just took off running and he never ever looked back.

About 20 minutes later Big Cliff came to talk to Black about the strange episode that he had just now encountered inside of the down stairs bathroom. Big Cliff told Black that what he just witnessed was daddy giving himself the medicine that the doctor had prescribed and he had to take it with the needle. Black was really starting to sense that his father was just telling him a big lie. Big Cliff asked Black did he understand what he'd just told him. Black just looked at his father and just shook his head up and down so that he could get rid of his father.

Then Black had remembered that he had Chrissy on the phone with him. Chrissy had been calling Black's name for a minute or two, but he was caught up in the past run-ins with his lying butt father, and he didn't even hear Chrissy calling him. Black was caught up in how his father had tried to deceive him. Black came back to his senses and reality was that his sister was on the phone line with him. She asked Black was everything okay with him and why he didn't answer her when she was calling his name. Black told her that he was good and that he had just had a quick flash back to when she had asked him why he didn't hip her to the fact that he was getting ready to have a little shorty. Black's mind had drifted back to that old story and time that he told Chrissy about him catching their father with the needle stuck in his arm, in the down stairs bathroom.

Black asked Chrissy, "Do you remember me telling you about that Chrissy?"

Chrissy said, "Yea I do remember you telling us something about that incident with daddy."

Black said, "Chrissy I was hurt back then that daddy couldn't be a man and tell me the truth back then. He lied to me big time with a straight face, and to this very day that scene just plays over and over inside of my head."

Black said, "That father of ours had more game with him then parker brothers, anyway, what's up with you Chrissy?"

Chrissy responded "Nothing, I just now got in here from hanging in the market with Dia and the little one who's on the way, and boy before I forget, let me tell you when I was parking, your sister, no your drunken sister pulls up right behind my car and almost crashed the back of my car. Black, you have to get that girl some help, no some real help. She's drinking and driving around like a bat out of hell. I almost smacked Lisa a few minutes ago,"

Black asked Chrissy, "where she at now then."

Chrissy said, "she in the living room drunk, sitting there watching lifetime movie network, you already know that's all she do is turn on lifetime movies and sit there and cry through the whole entire movie. Black you know that mommy have been worried sick about you, when are you going to blow through this way to see us?"

Black said "I'll shoot through there tonight alright."

Chrissy responded, "Okay then Black Face talk to you later on," then they hung up.

Dia was enjoying every minute of the special time that Black was spending with her.

Black asked Dia, "What time do we have to be at the doctor's appointment?"

Dia said, "It is at 9:00am in the morning."

Black made real sure that he would always have his child's best interest at heart. Black made sure that he would be a better father figure then Big Cliff was to him and his sister's. Black promised that he would attend all of their doctor's appointments, no matter what was going on. Black was spending a lot of time at home with Dia and the un-born child.

Even though Black wasn't going out in the streets as much as he use too, his money and shop was still doing major numbers out of this world. By Dia being pregnant, it was also taking an effect on Black as well. He was starting to sleep a lot. Tony just couldn't hold the fort down as well as Black does it? Black finally got that special beep that he had been waiting for. Black waited for a few days to hear from the fakeness. It was Tony's special code with all #55555's behind the phone number. Black called Tony and he was sounding pissed because Black hadn't been out in a few days. Black told Tony that he would be out later on. Black already knew that Tony just wanted to hang out with him so that he could hook up with some girls, he didn't have no kind of macking game in his whole body.

Black ended their call with you I'll hit you up later on. Tony went and started counting up all of the money that he had collected over the past few days that Black hadn't been outside to get. It was just so crazy how much money this shop was bringing in. The 2 partners were millionaires and didn't even know it. It didn't take any time to get this status when you rocking that heroin the way they were. They were raking in so much dough that they now needed a money machine to count it up. Tony had started around 5:40p.m and he didn't get finished the total amount until 11:30pm. He always had to add something else to what he had to do. He had to go see this person and that person, instead of taking care of his business first.

His count was 4.4 million. Tony beeped Black so that he could come and put the money up in the secret vault. Tony had to admit it; Black was the best ever when it came to making that money and getting them girls. Black was what people would call Peddi & the Brain, all wrapped into one body. Black's mind is sharp and out of this world. He had to stay sharp living and getting all of this money like this in the #1 Heroin Capital in the world. Only the strong survived in this town. B-More is a very tough place to live; there are a lot of go getters and go hard dudes in B-More. A person gots to B-More careful in this city. These mean streets will swallow a person up so fast that they'll be dead before they even hit the ground. Black loved these mean streets of B-More, his partner or maybe even part owner of these streets, at least that's how he feels. Black is no doubt the man and he's at the very top of his game. One day, while riding down Whitelock St. where it's supposed to be an understanding of some kind of federal investigation by the fed's, someone just comes out of nowhere and starts flagging Black down and when he finally pulls over to see who it is, Black just smiles and appears to be very happy to see his old connect.

The first person to ever give him his first break in the game, Apple Sider walks over to Black and shakes his hand.

Apple Sider said, "Yo Black, I see that those rainy days have changed into a lot of happy ones for you over the years."

Black just kept on smiling, then he replied, "Yo, Apple what's good with you my nigga?"

Apple Sider said, "Black I hear that you're the man who runs these streets of B-More now. I hear that you're like the new mayor around here."

Black just sat there and listened to Apple talk then he cut in, saying "So what up Apple?"

Apple just put his head down after seeing the once little kid that he use to give g-packs, 60/40 packs grow up and became the man right before his very eyes.

Apple said "I taught you well Black."

Black said, "Indeed you did Apple, I owe you for what you did for me a few years back. I remember them days clearly my nigga. I didn't have a nice house back then, we lived in an apartment where me and my 2 sisters had to share a room, no food, roaches everywhere we turned, mice ripping and running around in the house like they owned the joint."

As Black was sitting there remembering all of the bad times and the things that he use to suffer, Apple just sat there and smiled at Black because he never ever forgot where he had came from, plus the money didn't change Black like it does to so many other people. Its working on Blacks heart to extend his hand back out and help his friend to get back right.

Black said, "so what you into my nigga?"
Apple Sider said, "Man I fell off bad and I've been searching high and low trying to find someone to give me a helping hand, but everyone just keeps on spinning me like I'm some kind of top. Yo, Black I have one last shot before I have to get down for mines by any means necessary. Black my last hope, can you help me to get back on my feet again?"
Black looked into Apple Sider's eyes and said, "No questions. Yo I got you something really proper. Give me a few hours and meet me right back here at 9:00pm tonight."

Apple Sider didn't have a dime to his name; he was really doing bad right now. He hadn't ate in a few days now, his stomach was hurting so bad from the hunger pains, but right before Black pulled off from Apple, he reached into his pocket and peeled off 5 $100 dollar bills and gave them to his man/ old connect. Apple Sider just looked at Black and started crying.
Black said, "here my nigga, take this get yourself together and I'll see you later on."
Apple Sider just looked at Black and started crying. Black responded by saying, "yo, you taught me that the top feels so much better than being on the bottom, so much better."
Apple said, "I know that feeling my nigga, I'll see you at 9:00pm."

Black said, "I'm here now for you like you was for me, see you at 9pm sharp, so that I can help you to get back on top again."

Black smiled, beeped his horn and pulled off. He was pushing his silver 8501 BMW on this day. As Black pulled off he glanced down at his iced out presidential Rolex watch to see just how much time he really had left before he had to meet back up with Apple Sider again. It was now 2:07pm which gave Black like 7 hours to play with. Black couldn't believe that his man Apple had fell off like he had, but he always remembered that saying Apple had always told him about them rainy days. Black had even experienced it one day as well when he messed up all his money and he only had that $250.00 dollars left to climb his way back up to the top. He remembered his other dude T-Mac too, who had helped him to get back right again. Black was starting to really wonder what was up with T-Mac and was he still doing good or not. He was sure to put out an APB on T-Mac so that if he needed some help, he could extend his hand out to him as well.

CHAPTER 4

Black had a lot on his mind after seeing his man down in the slumps like he was, so he was just riding around trying to clear his head and was enjoying the sight of this nice day. As Black was driving he spotted this bad lil shorty. Black didn't know her yet, but he was on her heels and would soon learn of who she was in a matter of minutes. As Black pulled over and parked to wait for this girl to walk in his direction, they made eye contact when she reached Black. He was just standing there smiling from ear to ear.

Black said, how are you doing today Miss Lady?"
The girl replied, "Find and you?"
Black said, "I would be much better if I could take you out?" The girl just smiled at him, she was feeling his swag and sense of humor already. Black asked, "So what's your name sexy lady?"
The girl said, "My name is Bay-Bay, and yours?"

She had been praying for this day to come so that she could meet the infamous Black in person and somehow be a part of his fleet of women.

Black said, "Everyone calls me Black."
Bay-Bay said, "Oh, you Black, I've heard so much about you, but I've never been able to put a face with the name that I kept on hearing about, but now I see what all the fuss was

about."

Black replied, "I see that your sexy face fits your name."

Bay-Bay just stood there smiling at him. Black then asked her, "So Bay-Bay do you have a number where I can reach you at?"

Bay-Bay reached into her purse, pulled out some paper and a pen and she wrote down her cell phone number, pager number and house number. Bay-Bay gave Black every number that she could be reached at because she didn't want to ever miss his calls, whenever he did decide to call her, she wanted to be available. Black tore off a piece of paper and he wrote his pager number down for her. Black said his good byes to her and hopped back into his car and just before he pulled off he turned around to get a good look at her phat butt and as he already knew it she was thick to death.

All Black could do was lick his lips, she turned around and caught him staring at her butt, she played it off and began to wave good bye to him as he began to pull off. She was dark skin, 26 years old, 5'7 150lbs small waist, small feet, and she's very sexy in her own little ways, she has 4 crown golds in her mouth, which enhances her beauty, she's thick to death, fly as a bird, and she has nice long hair. Bay-Bay kind of puts you in the mind frame of Foxy Brown, and she has a walk that's out of this world. She always turned a lot of heads; her walk is so mean that she always seems to cause a traffic jam. Black stayed knocking women, with him it's an art, he just so smooth with how he lays his charm on the women. He always tells himself, I'm the man! Black has always said silent prayers to his Lord and Savior Jesus Christ. He also knows in his heart that it's never ever him that do anything that's happening good for him, living good, eating good, dressing good, and he knows it's the Holy Spirit working inside of him.

Its' a true blessing to be who he is, it's even times when he just rides around and prays and speak to God for many hours, just thanking and praising Him for everything. He's very thankful that he's not hurting anymore, hungry no more, and always keeping him so fly. Whenever he would get finished talking to God he always close off with in the name of Jesus Christ Amen! Black knows that he has to get his self-legit and leave the drug game alone. There's no future in the drug game at all, if your smart enough, you would get in if that's what you choose to do and get out if you're lucky enough too. Some people make it and some don't. Its only three ways in the drug game.

1. You either do it big, make money, enough money to go out legit.
2. Get money and get killed in the process.
3. Or you either make money, make a name for yourself, and then go to jail to spend the money that you broke the law for with the government on their little food markets that they have set up in the fed's called commissary, or on their high phone calls and pay them high fines.

So ask yourself, really is selling drugs really worth it? Black was heavy in his thoughts after he had just got done praying. Black was really trying to find a way to go legit. This had become his main focus, while driving around, Black's pager went off it was his girlfriend and soon to be baby mother Dia.

CHAPTER 5

Black called Dia right back. The phone rang 3 times before she answered it.

Dia answered the phone, "Hello, in her sexiest voice that she could muster up."

Black said, "what up Boo-Boo, you need something."

Dia said, "Yes, I need you inside of me, the baby is hungry, so can you come and feed us, some of that big Black, long snake of yours?"

Black just fell out laughing at how silly Dia really was, but he loved her to death.

Dia said, "Naw, I'm just playing around, but when you're on your way home can you stop at the market and pick me up 2 jars of pickles please. I forgot to pick some up messing around with your sister Chrissy, the other day while we was shopping together, oh yea and I need 2 pints of ice cream too. Some vanilla?'

Black said, "Okay baby I'll stop by the market and pick that up for you right now, I'm on my way and don't have nothing on when I get there, I need to make love to ya'll."

Dia replied, "I think that I can arrange that for you daddy and they hung up the phone."

While on his way to pick up Dia's orders from the market, Black had caught a serious hard on from just the thought of him getting ready to make slow sweet love to his baby Dia. Black got the pickles and ice creams and went home where Dia was awaiting his arrival. Just as he asked of her, she was standing there sexy as ever, just as he asked her, she was butt naked as soon as Black came in the front door. Black was so shocked to see Dia's beauty, he dropped the pickles and the ice creams right there at the front door and started getting naked right along with her. Before she knew it, Black was all over her hot spot. He knew what to do to get her hot, kissing her on her neck always drover her over the edge, made her hot and crazy, He started sucking Dia's titties like he was a new born baby, like the one that she was carrying inside of her. Her coochie is soaking wet, dripping cum juices; her vagina is pulsating so hard that it feels like she's getting ready to explode right inside of Blacks' arms. Dia's going crazy; she can't handle all of this foreplay any longer. She just was screaming for him to put it inside her.

Dia said, "Put it in me Black right now, and hurry up baby."

Black just laid her down on the cough and inserted his "9" inches of hard wood inside of Dia's super wet, wet coochie. She began to start moaning his name so loudly that it was starting to sound like she was speaking in a different language or something. Black took his time making slow, sweet love to her; she was screaming and moaning so loud with pure ecstasy because it felt too good. Her words were

"Daddy, I'm cumming again, she repeated that same verse like 12 times back to back".

Every slow stroke that Black took inside of her hot, super wet coochie, it sent shock waves through her whole entire body, her eye lids had veins popping up which caused her whole body to shake uncontrollably, her eyes at one point had rolled to the back of her head. Dia started moaning out loud saying Black what are you doing to me baby, explain this pleasure to me baby."

Black just kept on stroking her. Dia said, "I love you Black, I love you so much baby, I'm cumming again, don't stop baby please don't stop, I need this to last forever, don't stop."

Black and Dia made love for like 3 hours, they made love in just about every position known to man, any and every way one could ever imagine. After they had finished they got up and went upstairs to take a shower, it was almost time for Black to go and meet back up with Apple Sider. Black was getting ready to leave, kissed Dia and told her that he'd be back in a few hours; on his way out he kicked the grocery bag that he'd dropped when he saw Dia's naked body. The pickles and 2 pints of ice-cream that was all melted, she was very upset just a little bit, that she had forgot about her cravings for that vanilla ice cream.

Black saw her moping, Black said, "Don't trip over that, just clean up the mess and I'll swing back pass the market and grab you 2 more pints of ice-cream."

He kissed her ever so passionately and then he rolled out. After ripping and running around it was now show time. It was now 8:25pm and Black had just 35 minutes left before he had to retrieve 200 grams of raw dope, he headed to his secret vault and got out $20,000.00 dollars in cash. He put everything into one of his black duffel bags that he used to carry his basketball gear in and he ran and jumped into his Jeep Cherokee truck. He was real tired of pushing the BMW, so he switched up on the ride. It was not 8:51pm and Black had 9 minutes left, but he was already in the area where he told Apple Sider to meet him at.

Black was pulling up beeping his horn for Apple, who was right on time as expected. Apple Sider was caught off guard with the all-white truck, he was expecting to see the silver BMW, but Black had switched up rides on him. Apple

Sider got into the truck he was smiling from ear to ear at how good Black was doing for himself and they drove off.

Black said," Yo, Apple, do you have a safe house anywhere?"

Apple Sider looked at Black and said, "I don't have nothing or nobody yo. Everyone turned their backs on me, and left me for dead, except for my grandmother and I just stay there every night until I can get back on my feet, you feel me?"

Black just sat there and listened to Apples' story and it was so sad to hear that everyone had left him for dead. It all brought back a flood gate of memories of when Black didn't have anything. The feeling was sick and he felt all of Apple Sider's pain. He even shed a few tears as he listened to him telling him how when he was on top everyone was around, but now that he don't have a pot to piss in or a window to throw it out of, nobody wants to be around or be his friend anymore, but I'll get it all back one day.

Apple Sider said, "Yo, it's just raining cats and dogs right now for me."

Black looked at Apple's eyes and he really could see the hunger and fire that was burning in them.

Black said, "Yo, I see that you are looking just like the Apple that I know and first had met. You all fresh to death right now my nigga, shinning like the star that you are. Yo, Apple, I saw that when I first pulled up, niggas was all up in your mix."

Apple replied, "Yea, I guess they see a nigga all fly and slick again, they think that I'm jamming again." Black said, "Yo, it's just so crazy how people can sense that you're getting money or not".

Apple said, "I guess they know that I use to have a lot of

money and if I get fresh, they think that a nigga back on again. That's a trip huh, Black?" Black looked at him and replied, "Yes, it is Apple, but are you really ready to get this money again?"

Apple Sider replied with tears in his eyes, "Yo I have not done this bad in a very, very long time, so yea I'm ready to get this money again, by any means necessary."

So, Black sat there listening to him talk and say this and that now Black wanted to test him to see what his words held. Black figured that he would test the waters with Apple Sider and see just how much every word that he just told him meant for real.

Black said, "So will you take a corner man job for me at my shop for $150.00 dollars a day?"

Apple looked at Black for just a minute and thought long and hard, and then he said, "For you Black I'd do anything to stay above water so when do you want me to start working?" Black knew from that statement that he'd just heard that Apple was really ready to get money again; Black pulled over and parked the truck.

Black then said, "Yo, Apple I would never ever treat no friends of mines like a corner boy, I was just trying to see was that statement you made to me about any means necessary real or not. I have something even better for you. You will be able to go and start up your own shop wherever you want to set it up at. Yo, look on the back seat and grab that bag, that's all for you."

Apple Sider asked, "Yo, what's this?"

Black said, "Yo, it's enough in that bag to make a broke man rich again. Black told him its 200 grams of raw dope and $20,000 dollars cash. Yo, take that and go bounce back up on your feet, once you get back right again then you can come back and holla at me." Apple Sider got out of the truck, shut the door and Black pulled off beeping his horn at him. Apple just stood there for a minutes, he was speechless, and just couldn't find any words to say to Black as he pulled off, but Apple's tears said it all for him and Black knew what those tears meant.

Beep, Beep, Beep, was Black last words to Apple Sider, it's now 10:15pm and Black was headed to the block to see his main man, but before Black could even get to the block someone was flagging him down with their flickering lights that was coming at him full speed. Black stopped the truck pulled onto the driver side of the car and it was Tony driving his baby mother's candy apple red Prelude and that's the reason why Black didn't know who was flagging him down, he was kind of happy to see his partner Tony feelings was mutual between the two of them.

Tony said, "Yo what it do?"
Black said, "you know it do what it do my nigga, what's the word?'
Toney replied, "when are we going to get together?'
Black responded "maybe early in the morning, I have to get Dia this ice cream and I'm heading on in, what you going to do?"
Tony said, "I'm just laying low, I got her car so that I can hide for the rest of the night. She's pissed off too, but I still love her to death."

Tony's baby mother was fine as she could be, she's 6'0 125 lbs. light skin, long hair, loving, pretty teeth, she's skinny, but thick for her size and weight, plus everything is tight, she has nice perky titties, and she jazzy, she loves to fight a lot. She and Tony have so much love drama going on, it's not even funny.

Black said, "Alright then nigga, I'll see you in the am. Peace I'm out!"
Black got home in record breaking time to chill out with the one woman that he really loved. Its now 11:20pm and

right before Black had a chance to get out of his truck his pager went off and he called the number right back, because the person who paged him, Black didn't recognize this new number, after about 4 rings a sexy females voice answered the phone.

She said hello?"
Black said, "Hello, did someone page Black from this number?"
The female said, "Yes I did."
Black responded, "So who might this sexy voice belong to then?"
The female answered, "It's your new girlfriend."
Black started laughing hard now, and said, "I already have a girl friend and I know her voice like the back of my hand, so who might this be?"
The female said, "This is Bay-Bay."
Black said, I was sitting hear listening to you and I thought that this was you, what it do Bay-Bay?"
Bay-Bay said, "Nothing I was just sitting here bored to death, so I was trying to spend some time with you, that's if you are not tied up?"

Black sat there and thought long and hard about how sexy and thick Bay-Bay was, he then caught a hard on just thinking about digging up inside of her phat butt tonight, but then he shook the thought off quickly as he thought about his girl Dia and going on in for the rest of the night, plus he didn't need another ice cream let down tonight, so he told Bay-Bay as a matter of fact, I've been ripping and running around all day like a bat out of hell, and I'm too tired right now plus I wouldn't want to just pick you up and not be at my full potential , so I'm going to head on in for the night. This is your house number that you just him me from right?"
Bay-Bay said, "Yes, it is and you can call me anytime, well I'll talk to you in the near future, and they hung up the phone." Black turned off the truck and went on in for the

rest of the night. He walked in the house and Dia was still up laying on the couch eating her pickles and watching lifetime network.

She had caught a good movie on and she was enjoying herself. Did you get the ice cream Black"?

Black said, "Yes I got you ice cream big head."

Dia asked him, "Well can you put me some in a bowl please."

Black went and washed his hands, washed out a bowl and scooped the ice cream into her bowl. He went in and sat right beside her. Lifted her legs and laid them across his lap and rubbed her bell and watched as the baby moved all around and side to side, just watching as the baby moved all around really excited him to death, he just smiled to himself and thanked God for the blessing. It's now 12:40am and they both were tired so they turned off the T.V. and headed upstairs to their bedroom.

They undressed each other, Black dozed off first, but Dia wasn't really all that sleepy, so she let him sleep, as she waited to please herself. She always took what was hers from him anyway. She made love to him in his sleep, all of the time. This is a regular routine for her. She would get him hard and ride him in his sleep. The scene was so crazy, how she did her thing, you would think that Black was wide awake, but he was sound asleep. Dia was riding Black in his sleep as if she was riding a horse. She was moaning Blacks name and cumming hard. Her juices were flowing as if he was moving with her. Dia knew how to make love to an unconscious man. She always knew what she was doing. Dia moaned and moaned for 30 minutes straight, she please herself and fed the baby some of Black's sperm.

Dia was so good at what she did; Black would bust a nut inside of her while he was asleep. Dia got her freak on whether he was awake or asleep, she got hers. After she finished stealing Black wood she went into the bathroom, took a shower and came back into the bedroom with a pale and washed Black up. Took everything back, brushed her teeth, got back into bed and snuggled right up under Blacks arms and fell asleep.

CHAPTER 6

Black woke up the next morning to the smell of turkey bacon, fried eggs, pancakes, turkey sausages, and some fresh squeezed orange juice that Dia was cooking for him.

Black said, "It sure does smell good up in here." Let me go hop in the shower real quick, get dressed, and eat so that I can go and meet up with Tony. He hopped in the shower, and 20 minutes later he was dressed and headed into the kitchen where she was awaiting him so that they could sit down together and eat. While they were eating, she told him what her plans were for the day. Her main focus was going to Toys R Us and do a little bit of baby shopping. He reached into his pocket and pulled a big wad of cash and handed it to her. Black then kissed her and he rolled out. Black left out of the house and hopped into his money green Q-45 with the grill on the front, with the matching gold and green 3 piece BBS rims. They sat in the living room and talked about everything that has been going on. Tony then informed Black that he wanted to take a trip with some girls and that he would have to oversee their operations.

Black was not surprised at all about what he was hearing from Tony, so he just sat there and listened to Tony ramble on and on, crying like a little wussy. Once he was done crying, it was now Black's turn to talk and wasn't' going to hold anything back from Tony, because Black is the man behind all that they have. Black built their entire operation from the ground up, from scratch, and now he was just ready to move out on his own anyway. Tony was a head ache, plus he didn't know how to get no money on his own and Black was getting ready to prove his point.

Black said, "Well Tony I see that you have your mind already make up about your trip, so I'll just make it even easier on the both of us, I'm going to take a chill pill as well, so why don't we just shoot over to the house and we just split the money that's in cash and the dope we have left. We'll just cut it down the middle and we go ahead on our trips."

Tony didn't see this coming, nor was he expecting Black to say what he had just said to him. Black's mind was already made up just as Tony's was, so all Tony could do, or say now was, I guess this is it then.

Tony said, "This is what you want?"

Black answered, "Yea, this is it my nigga, you a free man now, come on get in your car and follow me to the house."

Black was telling Tony to follow him to the stash house. They both rolled out, heading towards the stash house. Tony was so sick about this; he didn't have a clue as to what he was going to do now, especially without Black and his partner no more. They had approximately 20 miles to go before they would reach the stash house. As they came off of exit A2, they made a right and drove like another 8 blocks and they were parking in front of the house. Black pulled in first and Tony pulled in right behind him looking all mad as he walked towards the house. He looked back at Tony.

Black said, "You look like you sick or something, you cool?"

Tony's fears of losing Black's brains were all over his face. Tony said, "Yea, my nigga, it is because I want you to do as you well please without you ever having to wait on me or vice versa. I got big plans of my own anyway."

They came into the house to retrieve everything that they had left and put it all up on the table.

Black asked, "Yo, did you collect everything from last night?"

Tony replied. "Yea I got it all; we did something like $125,000 dollars."

All together they had 6 bricks of raw dope and 3.5 million dollars apiece, plus whatever else they have left down at the strip.

Black said, Yo my nigga, I'm done with this stash house too, here are the keys to it, do whatever you want to do with it." Black started walking towards his car, but then he turned around and stopped.

Black said, Yo so how long you going to be gone again?"

Tony, said, Yo, for real, I don't even know if I'm still even going to go now, but it was supposed to be for 5 days."

Black replied, "oh yea, and you can have that block too for yourself. I'm just going to start a new one up. I'm going to create me a new team of go hard goons."

After Black said all of that to Tony, he knew that it was all over with his relationship with Black.

Black said, "okay then my nigga, I'll see you in traffic, be safe."

Black grabbed his money and bricks put everything inside his duffel bag and he rolled out leaving Tony with his hands on his face not knowing how he was going to run his own shop. Tony couldn't cut no dope like Black could, he didn't have a connect or anything. Tony was through now. Black pulled off heading towards his new stash house. Well not really new, because he was already jamming, at his other undisclosed location that nobody else really knew about, but him and his new crew. Black was always a firm believer in covering your butt and your back, because there's always someone looking to take your shine, your place, and even your life.

So he was prepared for this move a long time ago. Black knew that Tony was like this from up on Whitelock St. Black got to his spot and emptied out the bag, put the bricks in where he kept all of his other bricks and put the money in with the rest of the money that he had in the stash. Black had so many of them things that it wasn't funny. He just left from this spot yesterday when he grabbed the 200 grams for Apple Sider and the 20,000.00 dollars. His motto was, you got to stay ready so that you don't ever have to get ready, and all he could think of now was getting his 2nd shop all the way on the map. Black's getting ready to drop a fresh bomb on his new shop and redirect all of the traffic from where he and Tony had the first shop at, he was getting ready to shift Tony's whole entire world into nothing.

It's just a matter of a few days and he'll have every last penny that him and Tony was making around on Pennsylvania and Bloom St. Black was a great master mind for real, he allowed Tony to kill himself with his own tongue. At times Black just liked to find time and sit around playing himself in a game of chess, he knew every move on the board was a vital move, just like in real life, the move that he just now made to mate his old partner Tony with. Black been had the board set up for Tony. You always have to try to be 5-10 steps ahead of any adversary that you're up against. He tricked Tony into selling his soul. Tony wasn't a real friend of Black's to ever begin with. Tony was always out for himself. He always tried to do everything in his power to get Black to allow him to meet his connect. He saw right through what Tony was up to and just to be sure of Tony's plans, Black tricked Tony one time and told him that he couldn't make it to cop from dude. Dude is who Black always called his connect around everyone.

He went on and put his trick into effect as he explained to his long time Texas girlfriend father that he needed a big favor from him. Black wanted Mr. Elfredo to pose as his connect and meet up with Tony and see just what kind of a friend Tony really was to him. Black paid for the whole sting, and he paid Mr. Elfredo $8,000.00 dollars in cash, just for an hours' worth of his time. Mr. Elfredo flew into the Baltimore City's BWI airport 2 days ahead of schedule so that Black could run over the whole entire plan to bring out the snake if there was one lurking inside of his relationship with Tony. Black and Mr. Eldredo had a lot of fun together, plus they even talked a lot about his daughter Athenna still being in love with Black.

As the day for this meeting started to close in, Black kept on telling himself that he was just being too paranoid and that Tony would pass this test, but knowing that Tony's greed would soon tell him what he really wanted to know about him, his fate of why he couldn't even trust in Tony. This meeting will either pull Black away from Tony or it will bring them closer. Black knows that he's just too good for his own good, but real fake nigga's what you witnessing, they wish like hell all of the time to be like Black so much, yea its crazy but this is the way that it is.

Black called Tony and said, "Yo, I need you to go and meet up with dude because I have to go to a doctor's appointment with Dia." Tony knew that it was a lot of truth to this statement because Black doesn't ever miss any of the baby's appointments, for no reason. Black had his fishing line so deep inside of Tony's nose that he couldn't smell a set up if he chose to tell him it was a trap. Black just wanted to know for sure how far money and greed would break up a friendship. He would soon learn his lesson in the morning when Mr. Elfredo wears his wire and recorder. Every word that's spoken at this meeting in the morning will be recorded. Black was laying in the house with Dia that night and for some strange reason he couldn't sleep, this meeting in the morning was really eating at him bad and Dia sensed that something was really wrong and bothering her man, so she asked him even though she knew that he was going to tell her that he was okay.

Dia asked him, "Baby is everything okay with you?"

47

Black just smiled at her, pulled his self-up and hugged her real tight and said, "I'll know in the morning baby", and they dozed off. Black threw her for a loop with that statement, because she really just thought that he was referring to the doctors' appointment going great, but little did she know it was the meeting that had him stressing. Early that morning as they were preparing to take a bath together, Mr. Elfredo had a room downtown at the Ritz Hotel. Black decided to call Mr. Elfredo at the hotel room.

Ring, ring, ring, Mr. Elfredo answered "Hello?"

Black said, "What's up Mr. Elfredo, was it all a go and was everything still on point?"

Mr. Elfredo replied, "It's all a go."

Black said, "Okay then, you have to meet my partner Tony down town at the Fisher's Men Wharf. It's right off of I-95 south highway. I'll see you in a little bit, peace and they hung up."

Black then called Tony who answered the phone on the 1st ring, he was sounding so happy like he'd just hit the jack pot or the powerball or something. When Black called him, he could hear the excitement in Tony's voice.

Black asked, "Yo, Tony you ready my nigga?

Tony answered him, "Yo, I've been awaiting this day forever and Black snickered saying to himself, me too."

Black said, Yo, so I take it that this is the biggest day of your life?"

Tony smiled and said, "It sure is Yo."

Black then said, "Yo, tell dude that I said, I send my love and he'll automatically know that you're my man. We need 100 kisses no lip stick and he'll know that I want 100kilo's no cut. Yo, handle your business my nigga and let's get this money and take over the streets B-More. I'm out Yo, dude at the Wharf waiting on you in the back to the far right wall, stick to what we talked about, and never discuss anything that we never talked about and nothing that he doesn't ask you about. Tony do you really understand what we have talked about?"

Tony said, Yea, I understand Yo, I'll holla at you later on, peace and they disconnected."

Black and Dia went on ahead and got into the tub together, but for some reason Dia's beauty looked like she had a halo glow all around her shining brightly and it had Black wanting to make love to her so bad, but he was stuck because she couldn't have sex right then because she had to go to the doctors, but Black had almost forgot all about that and that they had to go to the doctors. The doctor had to do a check on Dia and it is called for the doctor to examine her insides and if Black was to cum inside of Dia the doctor would be able to tell. She couldn't have sex, but her mouth was just as good, so she please her man by swallowing his "9" inches down her throat. Dia could work wonders with her tongue and her jaws, she had his eyes in the back of his head, with his toes curled up, nutting all over and down her throat. Dia was so caught up in sucking him off that she didn't even feel his wood pulsating inside of her mouth and she swallowed every last drip drop of his cum.

Black said, "Dag baby you have the best dome in the whole wide world, and you deserve a championship head ring." Black just sat there and laughed his butt off after he'd just busted off inside of her mouth. Dia said, "well Black where is my ring at then?"

Black said, "I'll get you one made."

They washed up, got dressed and went to get into Dia's white Benz. She pulled off in route for the doctors. Blacks mind drifted off to how this meeting with Tony and Mr. Elfredo would turn out. Mr. Elfredo was already inside of the Wharf awaiting Tony to show up. As Mr. Elfredo took a look at his watch, he noticed that Tony wasn't a good business man at all; he was already 15 minutes late. Dealing with a real connect, being on time was a must and being late was a sign of disrespect. Mr. Elfredo thought to himself... The real connects motto was to always be on time and sharp and prompt. Tony would have had a red flag already.

Mr. Elfredo said into a small device, "Tony is now 20 minutes late for this meeting." As soon as Mr. Elfredo had finished his sentence, Tony walked into the Wharf with 6 other dudes and was playing real big in front of Mr. Elfredo. Tony walked over to Mr. Elfredo's table and said exactly what Black told him not to say. Black told him to say 100 kisses, no lip stick Mr. Elfredo was trying to rehearse what Black had already said.

Tony said, "Black sends his love and that he needs 500 kisses and no lip stick."

Mr. Elfredo stood up and shook Tony's hand. Mr. Elfredo said, "It's a pleasure to meet you finally. I've heard a lot of good things about you. Black speaks highly of you. How is business?"

Tony replied, "You know my name and I don't have a clue as to what your name is Sir?"

Mr. Elfredo said, "pardon me, my name is Elfredo."

Tony then said, "Please to meet you Elfredo, so tell me what Black told you about me?"

Mr. Elfredo responded by saying, "Well Tony you know that I and Black go way back, but that girlfriend of his is really bad for business. She's slowing him down a little bit and I might even have to cut his tides with my family." Just as soon as those words left Mr. Elfredo's mouth Tony's mind went to racing big time.

Tony said, "You know Mr. Elfredo, I was just sitting here thinking that very same thing." Tony had a big ole smirk on his face. Mr. Elfredo looked at Tony with raised eye brows.

Mr. Elfredo asked, "So Tony what do you suggest that I do about Black then?"

Tony said, "Cut him off and deal directly with me, and I'll carry things to the next level for you and your family."

Mr. Elfredo asked, "So Tony is Black your right hand

man, and just before he could answer or finish his sentence, Tony cut him off."

Tony said, "Let's get this straight, Black use to be my right hand man. I hate Black and I'm taking over this whole operation. I know now that I have the right plug to do it with now. Mr. Elfredo, do you know how long I've waited for this very day to finally meet you on my own. Black thinks that he's the man in B-More City."

Mr. Elfredo cut in and said, "It's really undisputable Tony and can't no one take that from him."

Tony responded, "I can."

Mr. Elfredo said, "How can you do that Tony?"

Tony said, "Because I'm the one who runs the shop, collect all of the money, pay all of the workers, make real sure that things are on point and running proper, and in order, its all me. Black just cut the dope and pass it on to me. He's not any major factor in this operation no more and I want to do business straight with you and your family."

Mr. Elfredo said, So, Tony you're telling me that you're willing to cut your main man off completely?"

Tony looked at him and replied, "Look Mr. Elfredo, I'm the real boss and muscles of these streets and Black could never survive without me. As I've said to you, I'm the power and real brains, not Black. His girls are his only boss and that's his real problem, girls are being put before our business. Black will just have to take a hike and find himself another block to hustle on. So tell me Mr. Elfredo, do we have a deal?"

Mr. Elfredo was completely stunned and knocked senseless at what he was hearing.

Tony said," I'm the one who up, or should I say, raised the numbers on the kisses to 500, no lip stick. He keeps on wanting only 100 at a time, so do we have a deal or not?"

Mr. Elfredo reached into his pocket and gave Tony his business card. Mr. Elfredo said, Tony before we part ways, give me your number so that I can give it to my family and we will be in touch with you. Are you sure Tony that you can move 500 of them things?"

Tony said, "I can move 500 of them things with my eyes closed."

Mr. Elfredo said, "Well I guess this is it then, oh yea before I forget, tell Black that his services are no longer needed. I finally found a reliable replacement whose shoes are way bigger than his, as a matter of fact that is 400 times more powerful than his are. Well Tony I'll give you a call in a few days and they stood up, shook hands and ended the meeting."

While at the doctor's office, Black's pager went off with the very same phone number that was from Bay-Bay's house. She was really trying to get up with Black bad. He had never even touched her, but she was very infatuated with him just because he's a very smooth and charming dude. He seems to have halo all around him and he's captivating all of the women. Everything went well with Dia and her check up with the baby. She was getting so big that people thought that she was carrying twins, but she had only one fetus growing inside of her womb. She didn't want to drive after the exam, so Black drove her car while she leaned her seat back so that she could just relax and listen to her song I'm so into you by Tamia.

Dia said, "Black this is my song right here, this was made for us, Black you are my all in all and she reached over and she turned up the volume to full blast and started singing along with Tamia."

On their way back home she told him that she was craving for some French fries and chicken nuggets from Mickey D's, so he drove through the drive thru to place her order. Black pulled up to the voice box. The voice box came to life and said, "Welcome to Mc Donald's may I take your order?"

Black placed the order, and then the voice box said,

"Will that be all Black?"

The sound of the girl's voice working the window caught him off guard, but he wondering who the voice belonged too. Black said, Yea that's all and he drove around to the girl's window to pick up and pay for the food. He kept on wondering who this girl was that knew him from behind the intercom."

Once Black pulled up to get the food and pay the girl, she waved him off. The girl said, "It is on the house and she passed the bags to him."

The girl was one of Black's secret admirers, her name is Mee-Mee. He had his stuff on lock and key in every way possible, the money, cars, clothes, fame, and which ever or whatever these niggas craved for. Black drove and helped Dia to get her food. They were so in love with each other. She turned the volume back down. Dia asked him "what are you going to do for the rest of the day Black?"

Black said, "I have to go and meet up with an old friend of mines, why what you got going on today?"

Dia said, "Nothing really, I just wanted to go and lay down and chill out, watch a little bit of T.V. or just talk on the phone."

Dia didn't have a lot of girlfriends, she had just a few, Dia's little circle was very small; she could count on one hand. Black loved that about her, she didn't spread herself that wide. She really not a peoples' person and he's not as well and his circle was also very small, other than his people who helped him to get on his feet. Black vowed to never ever forget those people in his life, on his way up to the top. He pulled up to their house, parked and gave Dia the keys and he ran and jumped into his Q-45 and pulled off. Black was headed straight downtown to the Ritz Hotel where Mr. Elfredo was waiting to share the new developments about Tony's actions, and everything that was said and recorded at the meeting. On the way to the hotel Black pager went off again, it was Bay-Bay's house number again. Black called her right back, the phone rang like 3 times and a sexy voice answered the phone. Bay-Bay said," Hello?"

Black said, "What it do?"

Bay-Bay said, "Can I please see you today?"

Black said, "Sure, I'll call you as soon as I get done taking care of some business, okay, and they hung up."

Black was amazed at how Bay-Bay was on him, but his mind quickly shifted to how the meeting turned out. Black was getting ready to hear everything, every word, word for word. Black walked straight up to Mr. Elfredo's room, he knocked on the door of room 624.

Mr. Elfredo answered, "Who is it?"

Black said, "It's me Mr. Elfredo, Black and he opened the door and started shaking his head in disgust. Black asked him, "How did my right hand man do?"

Mr. Elfredo said, "it was not good at all, here take this in the other room and rewind it and listen to the tape, the entire tape, the entire meeting for yourself."

CHAPTER 7

Meanwhile Apple Sider had started putting his thing down again. After his last meeting with Black and receiving the 200 grams of raw dope and the $20,000.00 dollars in cash, Apple was all the way back on his feet. He had even went and bought a new car. He ran into a junkie who had a lot of different connections before he had fell off and started getting high as a kite. The junkie's name was Big Phil, he use to go to all of the high price and high profile car auctions, especially the ones the fed's use to sponsor. You could get a big car for a little of nothing messing with Big Phil, but he had let the dope take him all the way down. Apple saw Big Phil in his dope line one day and as soon as Big Phil copped his 3 pills of dope, Apple waved to him so that he could holla at him.

Apple Sider said, "what the hell happened to you Big Phil, how did it get this bad?"

Big Phil said, "Man my girl left me and I was all stressed out, then I met this little freak while I was riding one day and she changed my life for the worst and here I am. I've lost my entire family and everything because of these drugs right here showing Apple the 3 pills that were in his hands that he had just now copped from his dope line."

Apple said, "So you mean to tell me Big Phil, you lost your dealer license to cop from the car auction too?"

Big Phil said, "Yea I've lost everything chasing after this

dope. I never had no time to go and take the tests or renew anything, I just gave it all up, but I still have a good friend of mines who's in the business and can still get you whatever you want from any auction."

Apple said, "That's what's up Big Phil, who is the dude that you are talking about?"

Big Phil answered, "I have to run right now, but I'll be back in a few hours to set you up with my partner, and Big Phil hurried off to go and put his blast from the past up into his veins."

Apple knew that if Big Phil came back it was most definitely on and popping again. He would most definitely have something big to drive in no time. He just stopped there with so many feelings racing through his body and through his mind. All he could picture was how good his man Black had it, and seeing Black on top gave him all of the motivation he needed to stay on top of his game. He also remembered the small shorty that had walked to him that one early morning right before he had opened up his shop. It felt just like it was yesterday, he could even remember Black's little voice.

Black had said, "Yo, Apple what's up?"

Apple remembered saying back to Black, oh what's up Black, you sure out here mighty early aren't you. What's the occasion?"

Apple remembered Black saying to him. I'm ready to get this money." Apple saw the other day what he had created inside of Black. He was the one who gave Black his first packs; he helped Black to gain the status of running the streets of B-More. He was the person who never turned his back on him when he needed him the most. Black never ever would forget who had helped him to get where he's at in his hustling world. Black never will forget what Apple taught to him. Black still remembers who taught him about them rainy days. He really knows who helped him so that he could get his shine on, his first shine ever, his first $100,000 dollars, who helped him to get his shoe game up, clothes game, to be well groomed, and made a way for him to lookout for the people that he loved and cared so deeply about.

Apple even was the person who helped Black to buy his first car which was a new Nissan Maxima from V.A. Apple always told his self that karma was real and how you treat people will always come back good or bad. He always did well to others so there was no doubt in his mind that good would eventually show up to him. Even though Apple never gave Black no big weight and it was always 60/40 packs, the reverse karma came back in a different form, plus even greater for Apple. Help comes in different forms. Apple did what he could at that time. In return Black's reaching out because Apple reached out back then to him. Black gave up a lot of weight and cash, so being good to others rules. Apple Sider said this to himself and walked away smiling from ear to ear.

CHAPTER 8

As Black sat down to listen to this morning's meeting, his mind drifted off back to Whitelock St., where he had grew up at with the rest of the guys, Sampson, Chuck, Ricky, Bobby, Yummy, Tyran, Terrell, and Calvin. Black was wondering where they all was at as far as their money. Black's heart is pure, and strong, very giving. He wanted to see everyone shinning and getting money, but it always seems like everyone hates to see him doing good. He had a connect that was out of this world, and he could get all of them up to where they needed to be at, or up to where he's at in no time, but Tony made Black's heart so cold by him being so grimy. Everyone from up on Whitelock. St. always knew that Black was the man behind the project, and all of Black's business as well because that's how Tony rocks.

Tony always ran his mouth just like a little broad. Always bragging about how he had it going on when everyone already knows the real boss is Black. All of the guys are getting money up on Whitelock. Black had thought of everyone just doing their thing, but he kept on having bad dreams about Tony. He just couldn't' put his finger on what type of dude Tony really was, but he did know that he had a real snake on his hands. Black's mind started to clear up when he thought of his mother Penny. He had not seen his mother in a few weeks now and he made up his mind to breeze through there as soon as he got done listening to this tape recorder.

Mr. Elfredo walked in the room and saw Black in a trance, but the tape wasn't on yet.

Mr. Elfredo asked, "Black are you okay?"

Black then came out of the trance. Black replied, "yes I'm cool I was just in deep thought about a lot of stuff. Mainly up on Whitelock St. that faggy nigga Tony and then my mother came to mind. Have to swing pass there to see her once I hear this crap."

Mr. Elfredo said, "Well Black you know that I have to fly on up out of here in a few more minutes, so my ride should be down stairs. I'll call you as soon as I get back home. I'll tell Athenna that you said hello and that you send your love."

Black said, "Before you leave, no never mind, here take this and give me a call and let me know that you made it back home safely."

Black passed Mr. Elfredo 2 white envelopes. His eyes grew wide as moth balls as he examined the contents; it was all $100 dollar bills flowing out of the envelopes. He kissed Black on both cheeks, shook his hand and he left. That was a sign of love and respect. Black just sat there staring at the tape recorder as if it had a disease. Right before he could press play his pager went off. He checks to see who it was and low and behold it was Tony. Black nonchalantly brushed him off, but his pager went off again, and when he looked at the number this time it was his man that he had assigned to the search for his other old connect from back in the days T-Mac. Black put listening to the tape on hold for a minute and called Boo-Boo right back.

3 rings and Boo-Boo answered, "Hello?"

Black asked, "Yo, did you find Mac yet?"

Boo-Boo said, "Yea Yo, I found him, but it's not good at all, but I'll meet up with you later on tonight, and they hung up."

Black pressed play and the recorder came to life.

The first thing that Black heard was Mr. Elfredo's voice. The tape running. Mr. Elfredo said "Tony is 20 minutes late for the meeting, and a few seconds late he heard Tony's voice playing big.'

Tony saying," Black sends his love and he needs 500 kisses, no lipstick."

Black was steaming as he pressed the rewind button to hear what Tony said again. He heard Tony saying, "Black sends his love and he needs 500 kisses no lipstick."

Black stopped the recorder yet again, looked at his pager and started dialing the number that Tony had just paged him from, as he was getting ready to press the last number into the phone, a voice spoke to him in his mind.

The voice said, "Black don't blow your cover, you have the upper hand now, don't blow it and show your hand to Tony just yet, play your cards right."

Then Black hung up the phone right before he dialed the last number. He pressed play again and the recorder came back to life again with Mr. Elfredo again.

Mr. Elfredo said, "It's a pleasure to meet you finally. I've heard a lot about you Tony from your partner Black. How is business?"

Black then hears Tony respond.

Tony says, "You know my name and I don't even have a clue as to what yours is?"

Mr. Elfredo said, "Pardon me, my name is Elfredo."

Tony says, "Please to meet you Elfredo, so what did Black tell you about me?"

Mr. Elfredo said, "You know Tony, me and Black go way back, but that girl friend of his is really bad for business. She's slowing Black down a little bit and I might even have to cut his tides with my family."

Black was sitting there smiling at how Mr. Elfredo had set Tony up for the kill like he had. As he kept on listening he heard Tony again.

Tony said, "You know Mr. Elfredo, I was just sitting here thinking the very same thing."

Black was just sitting there listening to every word closely and he couldn't believe his ears, then Black heard more talking.

Mr. Elfredo said, "So, Tony what do you think that I should do about Black then?"

Tony said, "Cut him off and deal directly with me and I'll carry things to the next level for you and your family."

Black was fuming hard after hearing all of that from Tony. Black heard more.

Mr. Elfredo asked, "Is Black your right hand man?"

Tony cut back in and said, "Black use to be my right hand man I hate Black and I'm taking over this whole entire operation. I know now that I have the right plug to do it with."

Black just sat there with a smirk on his face and he vowed to never ever allow another scum bag like Tony to ever get close to him ever again. He kept on listening.

Tony Asked, "Mr. Elfredo, do you know how long I've waited for this day to finally meet you on my own. Black thinks that he's the man in B-More City."

Mr. Elfredo said, It's really undisputable Tony and can't anyone take that from him."

Tony cut in and said, "I can"

Mr. Elfredo responded, "How can you Tony?"

Tony said, "Because, I'm the one who runs the shop, collect all of the money, pay all of the workers, make real sure that things are running in the proper order, it's all me. Black just cuts the dope and gives it all to me. He's not a major factor in this operation no more, and I want to do business straight with you and your family."

Mr. Elfredo responded, "So what are you telling me Tony, that you are willing to cut your main man off completely?"

Tony said, "Look Mr. Elfredo, I'm the real muscle of these streets and Black could never ever survive without me. As I have said to you, I'm the power and Blacks not, I'm the brains. His girls are his boss's and that's his real problem."

Mr. Elfredo said, Girls are being put before our business?"
Black was heated about this entire meeting, but he kept the
tape rolling.

Tony asked, "So Mr. Elfredo, how do you think that I'm
right here now sitting here with you and not Black? His girls
always first. That's my block to hustle on, so do we have a deal
Mr. Elfredo?"

Tony continued, "I'm the one that took the kisses up to
500, no lip stick. He keeps on wanting to get only 100 at a
time, so do we have a deal or not?"

Black heard a little bit of fumbling around.

Mr. Elfredo said, look Tony you give me your number and
me and my family will be in touch with you soon."

Mr. Elfredo asked, "are you sure that you can move 500
kisses?"

Tony answers. "I can move them things with my eyes
closed."

Mr. Elfredo said, "Well tell Black that his services are no
longer needed. I have found a reliable replacement whose
shoes are 400 times way bigger and more powerful than his
are."

Mr. Elfredo continued, "Tony I'll give you a call in a few
days." Black heard them ending the meeting. The tape was
just running now and Black was speechless from hearing Tony
talk the way he had been talking about him.

Black just sat there staring into space, just thinking about
how he just masterminded this plan against Tony. Penny sure
did teach her son well. As smooth and smart as Black is, you
would think that he grew up with both of his parents in his life,
but Penny was his mother and his father figure. She's still
running the streets of B-More as well. She keeps her at least a
brick or 2 just lying around her at all times. Penny has a few
cars now and she now lives in the suburban area of the city. She
doesn't live in the small apartment building over top of the
little store on Reservoir St. called Eddies. Eddies was on

the first floor of the apartment building where Black and his 2 sisters use to live at. Eddie was a very cool and laid back type of landlord; he always looked out for Penny, even when she couldn't get all of the rent money up at one time. Eddie always had a good heart when it came to Penny and her family.

Black had kind of looked up to Mr. Eddie. She always respected him to the fullest. Black always had his mind made up, that once his mother Penny moved and got herself together that he would come back for Mr. Eddie. Black knew that once he got his money up he had Mr. Eddie on his list to do, and he was going to bless him really well for what he did for him and his family when they needed the help. Mr. Eddie was the one who did it for them. Black never ever forgot about what he'd planned to do for Mr. Eddie. He was a pretty decent land lord, let the games begin. Tony never really knew the real reason why Black never came back around Whitelock St. anymore. Tony was just so blind by his own greed that he didn't see his plan back fire on himself until it was too late, all over and done with. As Black left the hotel room, he was just smiling to himself. His plan was to prove to Tony that indeed he is the man, and that it is the other way around, that Tony will never ever again make another dollar like he was when he was working with Black.

Tony had even tried to use the card that Mr. Eldredo had giving to him, which was a number that had been out of service. Once Tony heard the recording come on, he couldn't believe his ears, so he redialed the number on the card again and it repeated the very same thing again. Tony knew that it was all over with now. He still had one last shot in the dark, which was him hoping that Mr. Elfredo might still call him in a few days. Black was leaving the hotel he called up his head crew member, Cross who ran the other shop on Gold St.

He dialed Cross's number, and a sexy girls v o i c e

answered on the 2nd ring. "Ring, Ring, "Hello?"
Black asked, "Is Cross around?"
"Who is this?"
"This is Black."
"Oh, hold on Black, she said, Cross come and get the phone, its Black on the phone, hurry up boy, and Black please forgive me, I didn't even know that this was you, I'm sorry, "
Black just laughed, Black said, "shorty it's all good,"
Cross picked up the phone, "What it do?"
Black said, "You know what it do, it do what it do, what's up Yo?"
Cross sneezed and said, "Well Yo, I'm getting ready to open up shop, so we can take down like the world trade center did."
Black responded "Well I have something way better for the both of us today, Yo go through the block today and give out like 4,000 testers, pay all of the workers for whole days' worth of work give the worker's their 2 jumpers for the morning, afternoon, and night joints. Give everyone $150.00 dollars for the corners, pay the hitter's $250.00 dollars and close up. Tell everyone that shop will be back open again tomorrow and spread the word that we're giving out testers again in the morning also, so tell them to tell everyone that Thug life will be out."
Cross asked, "Is everything alright Black?"
Black said, "Yea, it's all good were getting ready to shut the whole City of B-More down, and I mean every other block will feel my wrath, Tony will feel my vengeance. He will pay retribution for his wrong doings. Are you really ready to get this paper Baby Boy?"
Cross said," I never been more ready in all my life."
Black said, "3:00pm. Should be the best time to rock and roll with the testers because that's when the police are changing their shifts and we'll have no interference, or no kind of spoiling of our mission to hit every last person who shows up for these T's. Yo what up with the rest of the ruffians?"

Cross said, "Yo they are all chilling, waiting to come out, but that's on hold until tomorrow, after we give out the T's right?"

Black answered, "Yea, but everyone can just go down V.A. and cop some whips. Cross then said, "That's what's up Black that sounds like a good plan too, I'll holla at you in a New York second."

Black said, "Peace and they disconnected."

CHAPTER 9

Big Phil just came back around to see Apple Sider and introduce him to his friend Carletto. Carletto was pushing his brand new 600 Benz, just chilling. Apple walked up to where they had parked the car at.

Apple said, "Man Big Phil I'm sure glad that you didn't forget about me."

Big Phil responded, "I told you that I would be back didn't I?"

Apple said, "Yea, you kept your word Big Phil, is this your friend that you was telling me about?"

Big Phil said, "Yea this is Carletto and this is a really good business client of mine. Carletto this is my friend Apple Sider that I have told you about."

Carlettto shook Apple's hand and asked him. "What is it that you are trying to do?"

Apple Sider said, I'm trying to do it big right now for me and my peoples. I need to come through B-More and give these niggas a real show."

Carletto said, "Well with me it don't take a lot of money to get a nice car from me, with me it's like taking candy from a baby. I got like 10 stacks to play with right now."

Carletto said, "Well I can go and get you a nice black on black quarter to 8."

Apples' eyes were wide open now, knowing just what Carletto was telling him that he had for him. He was telling

Apple that he had 745 BMW shiny black with the black interior.

Carletto said, "I have that just sitting right there in my drive way for you. It's been parked there for a week now."

Apple asked, "So when can I get it then?"

Carletto responded, "I'll meet you right back here in the same spot in 1 hour. When I get back we'll do the paperwork so have me all of the right info so that I can put the car in someone's' name. I'll have the name of my cousin by the time you get back, plus I'll have all of her information as soon as we get back, plus I'll have that cash for you."

Carletto drove off and left Apple standing right where he was at. He walked off heading to the house and sat down on the steps. Apple's mind just kept on drifting off, back to the lessons he'd taught Black about them rainy days, and he turned right around and fell victim to the very same kind of days. Apples' problem was that he had started spending way too much money then what he was actually bringing in, partying hard, taking too many trips, taking care of too many girls and fake friends. He was making it rain in the clubs, buying the bar out as well, but he had lost focus, forgot his own rules, and he never thought that them rainy days would ever catch up to him. He was sitting there in deep thought about his life and what he wanted to do from this point on out. He now knew how it really felt to have everything one day and lose it all the next. All in a blink of an eye, he felt blessed that he never gave up on himself like so many others have.

Some people just give up, quit and start getting high to try and ease their pain, but that's most definitely not the right answer at all. The smart answer is for people to remove their pride and ask for some type of help. That's what a real man/woman will do. He gets up off of the ground and he asked for some help.

Apple just said a silent prayer and thanked God for freeing him and for carrying him through the sand. He thanked God for not allowing him to start getting high like so many others as well.

Apple was sitting there in super deep thought, when Tarsha walked up beside him and slapped his leg.

Tarsha said, "Boy you look like you in space somewhere."

Apple said, "what are you doing up on this block that's drug infested girl."

Tarsha said, "I just stopped by to see if you were okay? I haven't heard from you or seen your butt in a few weeks now. I went past your grandmother's house and she told me that you moved out, and I was so worried about you, so I came up here looking for you to see if you wanted my S.I.S. check? I just got it in the mail today. You know that I really love you Apple, always have and you can have my last penny. I see all of your so-called friends have turned their backs on you now, but I guess the rain has that kind of effect on people huh? But you already know that I'll always hold you down and hold onto your hand and withstand any kind of weather with you Apple. Rather you're on top or on the bottom I'm here until the storm and bad weather is clear." She bent down to where he was sitting and kissed him, she whispered into his ear, I guess your so-called girlfriend left you too? Apple I've always been here for you and I'll always hold you down just like how Bonnie held Clyde down. So where are you staying at now? I really want to be with you wherever you're staying at, and if it's in a shelter then I want to be right with you, lying beside you. So Apple can I be with you and be your woman? She had tears in her eyes. I know you don't have nothing and I want you to know that I really love you even when you are broke and don't have 2 pennies to rub together. She was crying, he looked at her with tears in his own eyes as well, because he knew that she was not out for no money, she really wanted to be here for him in a major way.

Apple said, "Yea Tarsha you can be my woman and you know what?"

Tarsha asked "What?"

Apple said, "I've never in my life heard anything this sincere, special, straight forward distinct, and your way is beyond the usual individual's. My grandmother was the only woman who stood with me, and now I have you by my side. Tarsha I'm good!! I don't need your S.I.S. check. Thanks for the offer. Plus, things are already back on point with me again. I don't stay in the shelter; I have a house now, of my own. I don't have a car yet. It's all good, we're getting ready to cop one in a few minutes though. Plus, you can come move in with me this is perfect timing right here for real. Do you have any idea how hard it is to find a compatible woman like you, who don't care anything about what a nigga got or what kind of car he has?"

Tarsha said, "Apple you already know that I've never been into all of that materialistic stuff that will soon pass away."

Apple said, "I know that much about you, but look, I need you to stay right here and I'll be right back, I have to run and pick up this money for Carletto real quick."

Tarsha looked at him and said, "For who, but he was already running up the street, yelling for her to stay right there, just give me 5 minutes and he was gone."

Tarsha was a little bit upset and she just sat down on the steps and waited patiently for Apple to return. Tarsha was fine as can be, she was light skin, 5'3, 141 lbs., she is super thick with nice firm breast, she had hazel eyes that change colors according to the sun, perfect round shape butt cheeks, pigeon toe, with a gap. She's a nice dime piece; she stays to herself and loves Apple to death. Tarsha turns heads, everyone's head males and females. 5 minutes later Apple was riding back down the street on a brand new mountain bike with a Black book bag on his back.

Tarsha asked Apple, "What are you doing, you on your way to school with that book bag on, it makes you look like a college student."

Apple was getting ready to answer Tarsha back, but just before he could answer her and get the words out of his mouth, a black on black BMW had hit the block and all you could hear was all of the little children yelling and screaming that's my car, that's my car right there. Apple looked at the expression on Tarsha's face as she stared at the car. Apple looked at her and finished off what he was saying to her before he ran off to go and get the money.

Apple said, "Let me say this and we can go and get our car."

Tarsha said, "I don't have nobody to answer to and I want to stay with you and be the queen of the new domain or should I say palace."

Apple said, "Tarsha you are crazy boo, you do have a license right?"

Tarsha said, Yea I do but I don't have a car yet I told you."

Apple said, "Look right there, you have one now."

Carletto pulled over and parked. Carletto and Big Phil got out and walked over to where Apple was standing at with the bike.

Carletto asked, "Apple you like that?"

Apple was trying to talk but he was cheesing too hard, but managed to say yea let me get that joint."

Carletto said, "you have to fill out the paperwork right here for your new toy."

Apple told him to give the paperwork to Tarsha to fill out and get some insurance."

Apple passed Carletto the book bag that had the money inside of it. Carletto stood in the middle of the street, waved his hand and a women drove up the street in his Benz and Carletto and Big Phil got into the Benz and the woman drove off. Tarsha was at a loss for words, a little astonished, or amazed at what had just transpired right in front of her eyes. Tarsha couldn't believe that she had just put at 745 BMW in her name. Apple went inside of the house and got a butter knife so that he could put his temp tags on the car, so that they could ride, just him and his new girl Tarsha. He wanted to show her just how the new 745 BMW rode for real. Apple had made a tremendous come back, he's almost back the way that he used to be.

Apple said to himself, under his breath, "I've just now bounced all the way back now."

Tarsha was so happy for her man and she couldn't stop smiling. He couldn't stop smiling either. Apple and his woman was chilling, riding around getting their shine on, niggas was hating and looking like they had sour balls or lemon heads in their mouths. It was an atrocious or wicked sight to see. Apple has his mind made up, he knows that he really has to stay focused now and keep his eyes on the prize. His new shop was doing its thing, it was jumping and he was now stacking his money up like crazy. He has less than 2 more days and he would be finished selling the whole 200 grams of heroin that Black had blessed him with. From the looks of things Apple was most definitely in grind mode and so was his new team that he orchestrated together.

Apple had arranged a meeting so that he and his clique could put their minds together and design a good name for their dope shop. Everyone walked around thinking of different names from past movies, good movies that will set their dope apart from all of the other dopes that were in the city. Apple came up with the name and the name that he decided to use would most definitely describe him and all of the rest of his clique.

Apple Sider said, how about we call the dope bounce back?" I say that because we all are getting ready to bounce back." Everyone said in agreement, "there it is then bounce back."

They were all indeed getting ready to bounce back, all the way too. Apple just couldn't wait until these last 2 days were up, so he could hit Black up and show him what he had helped him and his new clique to accomplish.

CHAPTER 10

Black had just pulled up and was parking in his mother's driveway. Penny was just sitting there, chilling on her front porch, legs crossed drinking her beer and shaking her head with joy, gladness, pleasure, and excitement as her son walked up to her on the porch.

Black said, "What's up Ma?"

Penny was sitting there a little tipsy, off of the beer that she was sipping on. She's always real emotional whenever her son calls or comes around her. Penny had just started crying for no reason, just tears of joy because her son had stopped by and she haven't seen him in a while. She was talking and crying all at the same time.

Penny said, "Black I love you so much, why haven't you been coming around or checking in with me on a regular basis? Black you know that I worry myself to death about you."

Black leaned down and kissed her on the check and wiped her face, she had so many tears flowing, that she could fill up a river.

Black said, "Ma, I'm okay, chilling out, but I be needing to see you and see for myself that you are okay?"

Penny replied, "Black you are my only son and I be needing to hear your voice to confirm that my baby is fine. I know that none of these jealous niggas out here in these streets really like you. Black listen to me real carefully okay, oops my bag I'm a little bit drunk, I said to be real careful, and she started to laugh a lil bit at herself, but really Black listen to me baby. I don't trust any of these fools at all Black. I'm very sure that I already told you that I hate that faggot partner of yours Tony. I really do Black, be careful around him please. Black I'm always hearing a lot of real bad stuff about Tony. He's always sitting around running his mouth, telling a lot of lies and gossiping just like lil girls do sitting up in the hair dressers. With him it's always a whole lot of idle talk, vain and very foolish.

Everything he speaks on just be so worthless and don't have no meaning to it. He's always sitting around discussing ya'lls business with other people who be speaking on things that they don't even have a clue about. Black do me a big favor please and stop messing around with that circus clown Tony. Black let me let you in on a little secret that I've known since the day that I conceived you, meaning when I first became pregnant with you. Black you've grown up and became the man that I've always imagined and dreamed you would grow up to be and plus more. You have done it Black, you have proved that you can get money, you can get women, you can dress, you're a good father, you drive any kind of car that you want to, you can think, you can conquer success, you accomplished whatever you set your mind out to do, so what's next Black?"

What will my son set his heart on next?

Penny said, "Black get out of the drug life and try to live a real and meaningful lifestyle. You have plenty of money."

Black just stood there and thought about what Penny had just said to him. He carefully replayed her question to him inside of his mind, before he answered her back, Black said, "Ma, I'm almost ready to hang up this life, retire and pass my drug ring glove to these streets." She was very happy to hear Black tell her that statement.

Penny said, "Black you're a very sharp and wise young man, son just keep your eyes open and never ever give up. Black I've designed a few more laws for you and I'm very sure that you already know them. I'm almost ready to instill these laws into your heart.

What I have is simple. It's just things that we both already know, we just have to start applying them to our everyday lives, that's it. Black, But I haven't seen you in a few weeks, is everything still running smooth for you?"

Black looked at his mother with so much pain and hurt in his eyes.

Black said, Ma, how is it that you be knowing and feeling who is who?"

Penny just started staring at Black for a few minutes.

Penny then replied, "Black I know all things because I seek God's face daily, I fast and I pray. I walk with the Lord Jesus Christ!!!! Amen!! I ask him to reveal things to me and guess what?"

Black asked, "What ma?"

Penny answered, "God will show you who is who, and just about any and everything that you want to know, just ask Him and pray all the time. Black all you have to do is ask Him."

Black knew good and well that, what Penny was saying to him was all true; he just kept on trying to do it in his own power.

Penny said, "Black I know good and well that I have told you this emotional, heartfelt, sharp, very sincere, and extremely sad, but true story about me. When I was a little girl several times am I right?"

Black said, "Yes Ma, but can you explain to me what your past has to do with my life?"

Penny started crying a little harder now and he took a seat beside her, cuddling her, embracing her, comforting her, shedding tears with her, holding her very tightly in his arms as he whispered in her ear.

Black whispered, "Ma is not all that bad, is it?

Penny said, "I need you to understand Black, that you're a child of God and baby boy your most definitely destined for greatness. That was one of the things that was revealed to me in my dreams for years and years."

Black asked her, "Ma, what do you mean by that?"

Penny said, "Black man don't like you and he will never ever understand or be able to ever comprehend you. Everyone, well not everyone, but a lot of people will always think of you as being weird or unearthly, not normal, conceit, arrogant, to proud, or a person who just thinks that he's all of that. Black it was a man doctor that told me that I would never ever in my life be able to have any children. Black, man always makes mistakes and man is always wrong, but with God, He doesn't' make any mistakes at all. He's always right and God is always on time. You weren't supposed to be born into this world, you, Lisa, or Chrissy, but look at how wrong man is always messing up and saying the wrong things.

God blessed me to give birth to 3 different and very beautiful, healthy, and very intelligent children. God blessed us Black, He over threw everything that man said about me, you, and your 2 sisters. Black you're different from everyone else in this world; you just have to find out just what your true purpose is in life. You have to know this too. Black you're not a drug dealer God has something much greater for you then selling drugs. Don't allow the devil to steal your joy and happiness. You are setting a tone right now that you have the power to bring God's people back to Him. That's what we are here to do Black. We have a job to do Black, that job is to restore what Adam messed up by disobeying what God gave him power over. We are to go out into the world and to the nations and restore Gods words to the lost people. Black are you really ready to serve the living God?"

Black said, "Ma, I'll have to pray on this."

Penny answered, "Make sure that you do that my son. You're so unique and that's why don't nobody really like you, and you have to be really, really careful because even the people who don't even know you hate you. But, know this Black, they hated Jesus Christ first. Their reasons are that you're doing too much, and you are in their way. My son, God has a special purpose or should I say calling for you. What you have is a gift and a great talent. You have the ability and power to create and make things happen that the average niggas out in these streets can't do. You smart, eager, direct, and sharp as a hunting knife. A lot of people envy and crave what you have. Your swagger is just so confident and so superb, splendid, grand, and very, very impressive that it will always cause people to misjudge you as thinking that your way better than they are, but Black it's not none of what people think, its' all happening this way because God has shown you favor.

You know that I might be a little bit drunk or whatever you might think, but Black I'm telling you the truth. I've envisioned your life while I was still carrying you inside of my womb. Like your very first hustle. You are carrying bags all of them bags down at the shop, stop and save market. I use to come into your room at night. I've always saw that fire burning inside of your eyes. You had a glow that shielded you; it was a glow that hung around you while you were asleep. Black I use to watch you in your sleep for many hours and you know what I always saw while I watched you?"

Black asked, "what did you see Ma?"

Penny answered. "I saw my one and only son, my husband, my king, my prince, my best friend, my love child, my everything grow up and rise to the occasion, you took your opportunity all the way to the top with a hundred million crabs grabbing at your feet trying to always bring you down, but son you never ever looked back. You held your composer, stayed calm, and focused on the mission that you had set out to conquer. I sat there a many of nights listening to you talk in your sleep. You use to always ask where my father at. I'd sit there and silently answer your question, I'm right here my son. Our spirits were always connected and you would somehow hear my answer in your sleep, you would stir, smile and go on back off to where ever it was your mind was wondering to."

Black glanced at this watch and it was already 1:37p.m. He still wanted to be there with Cross and all the rest of his clique to give out the tester's at 3:00p.m. Black had a little bit of time left.

Black said, "Before I forget Ma, What's up with Mr. Eddie?"

Penny said, "I haven't seen Eddie in a while Black, what about him?"

Black said, "Nothing really, I was just sitting here thinking about everything, mainly all of the many times and blessings the many, many times he'd bent over backwards to help us out whenever you couldn't pay the rent or whatever was going on with it being late, Mr. Eddie was cool as a fan. He always showed us love Ma. Mr. Eddie always had our best interests at heart, plus he never taxed us or made you pay late fees."

Penny replied, "Yea, Black your so right about that, Eddie has always been a good man, ever since I've known him, he's always had a very good heart."

Black said, "Ma, you know what?"

Penny answered, "What Black?"

Black said, "I have a lot of love and respect for that old man, and I'm getting money now, we need to reimburse him, give him a really nice little gift."

Penny said, "Black that's a good idea and I would really love to do something for Eddie."

Black said, "Naw, I got it Ma. Once I do it he will already know that it's coming from the family anyway."

Penny responded, "Black it's so many good things that you be doing, it's so very hard to find good people like Eddie around in this day and time."

Black said, "So Ma, how much do you think we could give Mr. Eddie for all of the many times he's bailed us out and all that he's ever done for us?"

Penny said, "Black of all that Eddie has ever done for us, I could never ever put a price on it. Black you just have to do whatever you think is fair."

Black said, "About $250.00 dollars a month."

Black said, "What I'll do is just go and pay Mr. Eddie like we owe him in some back rent for 3 years. Ma, you think that's cool?"

Penny said, "Black I think that would really touch Eddie's heart to the core. It would most definitely show him that you really did appreciate what he did for us back then. By the way Black, how much money would that be that you would be giving to Eddie?"

Black went and got some paper and a pen and he added it all up.

Black said, "Ma, it comes to like $9,000 dollars."

Penny responded, "So that's for 3 years right? That will be Black because, it's more than 3 days in a week, so you would have to do 7 years, which will represent the 7 days that are in a week, so we will give Eddie a gift for $21,000 dollars."

Penny just shook her head at Black.

Penny said, "Black you never seem to amaze me, but what can I say it's the me in you."

Black said, "well Ma, I had a really nice time just sitting here kicking it with you, but I have to get up and out of this joint, so I can get over here and handle some business, so I'll holla at you a little later on, plus I'm going to shoot through to holla at Mr. Eddie and hit him up with that gift that we talked about."

Penny said, "He's going to love it Black."

Black kissed Penny and ran to get into his car. Right before he could get into the car good and pull off he heard her hollering for.

Penny asked," Black how is Dia and my grand baby doing?"

Black said, "Ma, there doing fine, I'll be sure to tell her that you asked about her."

Black beeped the horn and pulled off speeding, racing towards Gold St. to join Cross and the rest of his clique. While Black was racing towards his shop, his pager went off again and it was his other girl Bay-Bay. Black called her right back and she answered on the first ring.

Bay-Bay answered, "Hello."

Black said, "May I speak to Bay-Bay please?"

Bay-Bay said," This is me."

Black said, "What it do?"

Bay-Bay answered. "What are we going to do today?"

Black said, "Are you dressed?"

Bay-Bay said, "Yes."

Black then said, "Well I'm on my way to pick you up, be ready when I get there."

Bay-Bay said, "Alright then and they hung up."

Black already had his mind made up that as soon as they were done giving out testers they were going to jump right on the expressway heading to V.A. Bay-Bay would go with him so that she could keep him company while everyone else was going to cop a few fresh cars to play with. After all she is a nice dime piece that he could prance around with and let her strut her stuff while he just smiled at her. Black called Cross up to see what was up.

Cross answered on the first ring, "whose dis?"

Black answered, "What's up, how are things looking out there?"

Cross said, "Yo, it's crowed out this joint. It looks like 10 armies out here."

Black just smiled and said, "Oh word?"

Cross said, Yo, I've never seen this many people united together since Dr. King was living and they both fell out laughing."

Black said, "Yo, did you pay everyone on the roll and let them know it's over with right after this is all done, and that we will resume back on schedule in the a.m.?" Cross said, "Yea, Yo, I took care of everyone just like you said, but Yo, guess who just came up cruising by all slow checking out our scenery, and I mean looking hard at the crowds?"

Black asked, "who Yo?"

Cross said, "Your main man Tony, Yo, dude was looking like he just lost his best friend."

Black just laughed, and said, "Yo, I'm on my way, and I'm bringing this new dime piece through so that she can keep a nigga company. I'm on my way to scoop her up right now and I'll be right there, and they disconnected."

Cross didn't know that Black was getting ready to hang up, and he still carrying on the conversation until he heard the operator tell him, if he wanted to make a call please hang up and try the call again. Cross was kind of upset with Black because he didn't tell him that he was getting ready to hang up, so he called Black right back.

Black answered the phone on the 1st ring, "What it do?" Cross cut in and said, "Yo, after we get done giving out the testers were heading down V.A. right?"

Black said, "Yea Yo, that's the plan that's why I told you that I'm bringing the girl with me to keep me company, you dig?"

Cross said, "Aright then, I'll see you in a minute, and when we were talking a minute ago why you hang up on me?"

Black said, Yo, I didn't hang up on you on purpose, my bag."

Cross said, "Alright, then, peace and they both hung up."

Black pulled up in front of Bay-Bay's house and she was looking her very best, stunning as ever. Black pulled up beeped his horn once and she got right up, waved to her aunt and walked to the car and hopped in. Black looked at how gorgeous, splendid, dazzling, and hypnotizing Bay-Bay was looking today. All he could do was stare at her beauty and whistle to himself.

Black said under his breath, man she's a bad, bad chick. She closed the door.

Bay-Bay turned to Black and asked in her sexiest voice, "how are you today, Mr. Chocolate and she tapped his leg?"

Black said, "I'm doing alright and yourself?"

Bay-Bay replied, "I'm doing fine, now that I'm hanging out with you."

Black pulled off heading to Gold St. It was now 2:45p.m. On his digital dash board clock.

Bay-Bay asked him, "Do you have Keyshia Cole CD?"

Black passed her the remote control. Black said, "You

can do the honors."

Bay-Bay just smiled at him and hit the search button until she got the disc #35.

Black said, "She seems to be all of the women's favorite artist?"

Bay-Bay said, "I'm most definitely feeling Keyshia Cole's music, and she hit the volume on Black, and laid her seat back and closed her eyes."

Black looked over and took a peek at her. Black asked, "As beautiful as you are why you don't have a man?"

Bay-Bay opened her eyes, took a deep breath and said, "Because dudes these days play too many games, plus their not on no grown man level, so I just stay to myself."

Black asked her, "So what makes me so different from all of the rest of the dudes then?"

Bay-Bay said, "You know what? I've been asking myself that very same question and I have not been able to come up or put my finger on it yet, but it will come to me and I'll explain it to you."

Black just kept on driving until he saw all of the people that were out there waiting on these testers. Black just drove past Bloom St. where he had just saw Tony walking up the block that didn't have a single soul on it. Tony was furious when he arrived on his block to find out that every last one of his worker's wasn't outside that they were all up on Penn & Gold St. From where he was standing at, so he decided to walk up a little closer and get a better view of who this new dope belongs to and low and behold, just as soon as he took his last step, he had the clique who was creating all of this big commotion.

The first person who came into his view was Black standing there with his arms wrapped tightly around a girl that he had never seen before. Black was holding her from behind with his whole new crew surrounding him. Black was chilling enjoying the new scenery with his new head lieutenant Cross, and Bam-Bam was standing directly behind him, Day-Day stood on the left, Paydro and Mookie just stood on post watching everyone, guarding the head man just like if he was the President. Once Cross raised his hand in the air letting his workers know that it was time to let the show begin, 30 seconds later all you could see was mad people ripping and running, shouting Titanic's' "T's in the hole, and people were running from all direction. A few fell down, a few got ran over, a few was crying from the rush of the traffic of people trying to get that high. Free highs were the best highs. Tony did not have a clue as to what he was seeing, so he called himself trying to walk on over and join in where Black was standing at. As soon as Tony walked over close to where Black was at, Paydro and Mookie whipped out their guns and told Tony that the tester's where in the hole, not over here.

Mookie said," Yo that's far enough don't come any closer or I'll shoot you my nigga."

Tony's whole body went numb once they upped their guns; the sight of seeing them aiming guns at him deprived Tony off all feelings. His eyes were the size of a tennis ball as he tried to stay cool and calm. Tony was so scared and caught off guard, he was stuttering, I, I,I,I, I'm just trying to holla at my man Black for a minute. The two gun men didn't pay Tony no mind, or they weren't letting Tony say another word, but Paydro and Mookie raised their guns in the air and told Tony to get away or we'll start unloading on you right now.

Black cleared his throat and said, "Hold up ya'll its cool let him on thru."

They then put their guns away and Tony walked over to Black, scared to death at what had just taken place. Tony tried real hard to play it off like he wasn't scared, but Black knew that he was scared because while he talked to Black he was shaking like a loaded pair of dice.

Tony was talking to Black, but he never heard anything that Tony was saying to him because he was hugging up on Bay-Bay, smelling her hair which had smelled so good to him.

Her smell was driving him crazy. She smelled like coconut.

Black said, "Yo, Tony what can I do for you my nigga?" Tony said, Yo Black Bloom St. looked like a ghost town. Yo, someone else is trying to take over around here. Yo, these new people whoever they are can't open up on Gold St. This is our territory."

Black just stood there smiling at Tony for a few minutes. Black, said," Yo Tony I thought that you wanted Bloom St. All to yourself, you said that you do all of the work, you're the man, I'm nothing without you and I had to find another block to hustle on."

Tony's mind was racing 200 miles an hour now.

Tony said, "Yo what makes you say and think something like that?"

Black said, "Come on now Tony you know that I feel things and I know when I'm no longer wanted, so I'm being the better man, you can have that block, Yo, Bloom St. is all yours, do your thing my nigga, get rich or die trying."

Just as Black had got done talking to Tony, all of his workers came over to where they stood at. The hitter was reporting everything to Cross.

The Hitter said, " Yo, C we gave out every last one of them "T's" and it was only like a hand full of stragglers that didn't get one, but we made a very big statement today, you can bet on that, everyone wants the new Titanic. I told everyone again that we will be giving out testers again tomorrow at the same time as we did today and that shop will be open to cop right after that."

Black stood there smiling and watching Tony's reaction as the hitter was relaying what had taken place at the tester line, and Cross was laughing his butt off. Right before the workers was getting ready to leave and get ready for their big day tomorrow.

Black said, "Now before all of you all leave, I'm going to need all of ya'll to come back out here and meet back up at 10:00 p.m."

Black wanted to hear all of the talk and the results of

what people was saying and thought about the Titanic dope. Everyone said that they would meet back up at 10:00p.m. Everything seemed so sweet and normal that the hitter thought that Tony was a part of the Titanic team and spoke his mind. He didn't have a clue Tony wasn't a part of this crew.

The Hitter said, "Yo, we are getting ready to lock it down around here for real, niggas are going to feel this statement, plus wont nobody be able to sell nothing as long as were out here,"

Tony swallowed on his own spit hard.

Black said, "Okay, then 5-O's on the way up the street, so let's break this little meeting up and I'll see all of ya'll at 10:00p.m. Tonight."

Everyone said, "Yea we will be here."

Black responded, "Are all of ya'll good on money?"

They all told Black that they were all good and that they would see him at 10pm later tonight,"

They were all going to have a little bit of fun and enjoy the rest of their day off, the hitter said, "Yo, my fun will come as soon as we shut the other garbage dope shops down.

Black told him in due time, I'll see ya'll later on, were all headed to V.A. and we'll be back."

Black said, "Yo, Tony I'm out and I'll see you in traffic my nigga. Me and my crew heading on down to grab a few new cars, I would invite you to join us, but I know that you have your shop to run, so go ahead and get that money my nigga. I really love seeing you get your shine on."

Black turned around and kissed Bay-Bay. Black said, Yo ya'll ready to rock and roll?"

Black said, "Yo ya'll feeling my new shorty?"

Everyone turned around and said, "yea but do she have any friends for us?"

Black smiled and said, "Do you have any friends for the guys?"

Bay-Bay responded, "I might have something for ya'll, I'll make a few calls when we get back in town. She thought for a minute and said, as a matter of fact I'll call them on our way down to the car place. I got ya'll for real."

Black told Tony "Peace and they all walked away." Black and Bay-Bay walked and hopped into Black's car, while everyone else hopped into Cross's BMW station wagon. Black led the way heading straight down I-95 South. Both cars were balling down the highway. Black had a really good sense of revenge for how he handled the situation with Tony while the crew gave out the testers. Everything was just falling right into place right in front of Tony's eyes. Black indeed was the man. Tony had just now tried to realize that's a fact that he'll never ever be able to deny that Black is the most cleaver dude that he ever knew. Tony turned around and started walking back down to his block where a few people had started coming back around now that Black's crew had got done giving out all of them testers.

All Tony kept on hearing now was a bunch of people and stragglers who just kept on asking for the Titanic dope. Tony was a real true hater. Everyone who asked for the Titanic dope he would tell them that he never heard of it.

Tony said, "I have some good dope called Dot."

One of the guys who was inquiring about the Titanic went on ahead and copped 3 dots from Tony's crew because Titanic wasn't out and he had copped from them before, so he knew that it was legit. People all over the city of B-More was in an up roar, causing all kinds of disturbances for Black's dope. People everywhere, after about an hour, after the testers were giving out people was passing out from slamming the Titanic dope. A few people had over dosed, but didn't die or go all the way to La, La, land. Usually when people Od'd on dope, whoever is with the person once they go out, they get tossed out into the streets or into an alley way and left to die. Nobody died off of the Titanic dope today, because their partners were saving them, putting their buddies in tubs of ice, some put ice on the men's balls to revive them, making them drink milk trying to save them from the deadly dope of the Titanic.

Everyone who had received a tester of the Titanic came back chasing it; everyone was feigning for the dope that Black had cut this time around. They didn't want anything but that Titanic. The addicts were going Titanic crazy. Tony was out on the block harder than ever before now. The Titanic had started creating havoc for Tony's dope shop. It was really slow out there for Tony. He was actually trying to make different people, who asked about the Titanic dope, buy his Dot dope. Tony was starting to kick people up their butt's, beating them up because they wouldn't buy his dope.

Seeing Tony act this way was unreal to his workers. It had started getting so bad for Tony that he went and got his hitter for the Dot dope to post up and tell people that he had the Titanic dope. Tony walked up to every one of his workers and told them to lie and tell everyone that they had the Titanic and start yelling it out that they had Titanic dope and that they are hitting on Bloom St. The move he had just pulled was a very scandalous move and very disrespectful toward Black. Tony had his whole entire crew imitating Black's dope. Tony's crew had started jumping and doing their thing off of the Titanic's name. They had started to mimic Black's dope. From 5:00pm until around 8:30pm. Tony was using Black's name he made at least $25,000.00 dollars easy. Tony's crew had shut down at 8:30pm. He paid everyone; he was so furious that he just collected his money, left around Bloom St. and went home. Tony was so mad that he didn't know what he was going to do now. Mr. Elfredo still hadn't called him yet. He knew that once everything that him and Black had split was all gone he was going to be stuck, and wouldn't have any one else to cop from. Tony has never had a plug to cop from. All Tony knew from what he had encountered earlier on was that Black was most definitely out for blood and making his life a living hell fire.

CHAPTER 11

Apple Sider had finally taken his girl Tarsha to his new house. She was very amazed at the house that he had purchased. The house was in a very well kept, quiet, and residential area. Apple had his and her's parking space. She always knew that he had good taste, plus she love the area.

Tarsha said, "Apple I can sure get use to living out here and smiling at the same time."

Apple said, "I sure wouldn't mind having you living with me."

Tarsha left from down stairs so that she could go on her own little tour to look at the rest of the house which was very beautiful. The house had 5 bedrooms, 3 ½ bathrooms, nice size living room with a huge chandelier that hung from the ceiling, dining room was very nice and spacious, plus you could enter into the dining room from 3 different entrance ways, a very large den with a nice walk on balcony with a platform projecting from off of the side of the house where a person could see the river, nice big rocks and the ducks out playing, a huge basement that was fully equipped with a flat screen T.V. 50inches, a washer and dryer, a day room where he would just play video games, or play on his computer, a weight room where he stayed in shape. His weight room looked like an indoor Bally's fitness gym.

He also had a nice patio with sliding glass doors, a nice big front yard where he kept all of his dogs at, nice and shiny hardwood floors, wall to wall carpet in a few of the rooms, heating and air conditioning, nice storm windows and the house was mean and Tarsha called it the bomb. Tarsha fell in love with this house.

Tarsha said, "Baby we need to have this joint featured in the next upcoming cribs show on MTV."

When she walked into the master bedroom she just laid down on Apple's bed and made herself at home. Apple walked into the room looking at how sexy Tarsha was while she was stretched out on his California king bed. He caught a quick hard on instantly, he walked over to where she was lying at and he just started kissing her with so much force and passion that she just instantly grew hot and wanting to feel him inside of her lover tunnel. She had started stripping off every last piece of clothes she was wearing in record time. He looked at her body which was flawless and so well put together. Tarsha was a very beautiful woman. Apple knew that he had hit jack pot with her by his side. He peeled off his clothes in record time as well. They took their time with a lot of the for play, kissing, sucking all over each other's bodies, he was sucking her breast, her nipples were so hard, she started moaning with great pleasure as he parted her coochie lips, rubbing her clitoris up and down, side to side, just driving her crazy. Apple slid his middle finger inside of her wetness which caused her to hump on his finger, telling him to push it in deeper and deeper and never stop. Tarsha was so soaking wet that her coochie was farting, meaning that Apple was hitting spots along with the air causing her coochie to talk to him as she moaned his name over and over. Her juices where running all over his hand and the sheets, down to her butt hole and all over the bed sheets.

Tarsha said, "Apple I been waiting this moment for a long time baby give it to me, make love to me, I been wanting to be your woman baby, and I really want to live the rest of my life with you baby."

Apple started kissing her from neck on down to her

perky titties, down to her belly button, and he slid on down to where he was now tasting nothing but her sweet juices, flicking his tongue in a fast circular motion over her clit which sent Tarsha into ecstasy, She was cumming so hard that you could see her veins popping up in her yes, tears were running down her eyes from all of the good pleasure that she was experiencing for the very first time in her entire life. Tarsha had released so much cum that for a minute Apple thought that she pee-peeped in the bed, her moaning was endless and he had to get inside of her wetness, her love hole, and he wanted to feel her coochie muscles contracting around his wood.

Apple raised up as she was calling his name and he inserted the head of his wood inside of Tarsha's coochie. It felt so good to her that she was speaking in a language that Apple couldn't understand. Just hearing her speak like that made him harder and he was making love to her, she started calling his name, she was moaning louder now telling Apple that her body was all his. Their bodies was soaking wet from the intense love making that they were in. Both of their bodies were in great rhythm and to the both of them it was so good that it sounded like music to them. Apple and Tarsha humped and pumped for many hours, they both pleased each other and they made love, and made real sure that they satisfied each other and they both busted so many nuts that they lost count. They made passionate love over and over.

Apple said, "Tarsha you have some good loving girl, and I love you so much."

Tarsha just laid there and cuddled up under Apple's arm and smiled at him. She didn't want to move at all. She wanted this moment to last forever, they both were hugging each other for dear life, and she finally broke their silence.

Tarsha said, "I have always been in love with you, I don't ever want you to leave me. I want us to be together forever. I love you Apple, and I don't ever want you to forget this."

Apple said, "I love you too Tarsha,"

After that they both dozed off to sleep.

CHAPTER 12

Meanwhile word had spread like a wild fire that it was a bomb out on Gold St. Somebody new had come out with the dope called Titanic. The dope Black had was a killer; word had reached up on Whitelock St. as well, the Titanic had people coming from every side of B-More. The dudes up on Whitelock St. was still doing their thing pulling in a lot of money as well? Toney was at home taking all of his frustration out on his girl Shelly. Tony was beating her like she was a dude, so she did what she had to do to get this nigga up off of her. Shelly grabbed the sharpest knife that she could find, and she stabbed Tony in his hand really bad. Blood was everywhere. A nearby neighbor heard all of the cries for help that Shelly was screaming and she called the police. Tony was in so much pain from the wound that Shelly had done. Tony heard the sirens from a far off and he ran up out of the house with blood dripping everywhere and he left the house and went up on Whitelock St. where he thought that he would be able to escape what Black was bringing to him and his shop on Bloom St. Even all the way up Whitelock it was buzzing like crazy from everyone who messed with dope that it's a bomb down on Gold St. that's out of this world called the Titanic.

Everyone knows that Tony has a dope shop down on Bloom St. but a lot of people weren't sure if the new dope that everyone was asking for was Tony's or not, so as soon as he parked his car and walked over to where all of the action was taking place at, someone asked Tony was that his dope out there on Gold St. called Titanic? Tony was still being a hater and being sarcastic telling the people that it wasn't any dope down the way called Titanic, but he had Dot on Bloom St. Someone said, "We not talking about that garbage dot, we are talking about that new dope called Titanic, that's what we all want."

We all heard that dot is pure garbage and it's not hitting on anything at all. Tony was very upset that everyone kept on asking about Blacks dope and not his Dot. Tony was a nobody before he met Black and he's still a nobody now that Black has cut him off. Tony had a spending habit that was out of this world, but he was really getting ready to feel the effects of Blacks rage. In a matter of days Tony will have lost everything and every customer and so much money that he's going to think it's a great depression on Bloom St. All of his dot will soon fall because he can't sell anything, so the cut will eat the heroin up which will cause the dope that Tony has to go bad. In his mind all Tony can say is that Black has won again, but I'll get him one day. He was sitting there just thinking of Black's all time mottos, when he would tell him that its so many different ways to skin a cat and one way he just taught Tony without no force or getting violent.

Meanwhile Black, Bay-Bay, and the rest of the crew had made it to V.A. safe and had just pulled up and parked on the Eagle Motors Car lot. This car lot had so many different cars; all kinds of toys were lined up to choose from. It was so hard for the crew to pick from so many different types of toys. Black just watched his little crew drool all over the car lot. Bobby V. was always the salesman that Black loved to deal with, so he waited on the 5 of them to find something that they wanted to push through the city of B-More. Cross looked at them and told the rest of the crew that it was definitely their time to shine, so do it big my niggas. Black and Bay-Bay was just chilling in the car listening to the music, until she told him she was hungry, so he turned off the car and they walked over to the chicken place where they cooked some fine chicken. Black ordered a half of chicken with some of the best french fries that would put Micky D's to rest. Bay-Bay has never tasted the food from down here in V.A., so she just ordered the same thing that Black ordered. They ordered sodas and pecan pie for their desert. The chicken is off the hook up in this joint he told her as they were waiting for their order to come to them while they sat at their table. Black put his arm around Bay-Bay and told her that he really wanted to get to know her better. She's very smart and not just some average dummy plus she knows that as smooth as he is, he's got to have a girl, it's evident, but she doesn't care, she's just going to enjoy whatever little bit of time Black can make for her. She's cool with it, and she'll just wait for the perfect opportunity for when whoever his so-called girlfriend slips up and make a mistake and she'll be right there to replace her. Bay-Bay's mind stayed on enjoying her moment right now.

She's already heard that he has a lot of hoes in his stable already, she just wants to earn her spot and secure it. Bay-Bay is a very emotional girl and she doesn't even want to tell Black she's in love with him and she always has been. She just keeps a lot of things bottled up inside of her. He loves all of his girls too, and he does treat every last one of them with love and respect, especially his main girl Dia. He's been kind of under the low key act for real because don't nobody really know that he has all of these other girls in his life, at least that's what he thinks, but women gossip. It's in their make-up. He's just now starting to floss and show Bay-Bay off. The waiter walked over and dropped their food off at their table. She told them that she would be right back with their drinks. She dropped off their drinks and asked them would that be all?"

Black said, "Were good for right now thank you."

As they sat and ate their food, she took off her shoe and put her sexy manicured foot up into Black's lap and she began to rub her foot up and down Black's wood which caused him to stand at attention, get hard as a brick. He looked down at her foot in his lap and smiled and told her that her feet were even sexy.

Black said, "I see that you're a very good woman who's on top of her game for real."

Bay-Bay winked at Black and said, "A real woman must take good care of herself in all areas of her being."

Back at the car lot Los had just came back from test driving a candy apple 600 Benz and he was really digging this joint, while Day-Day was out test driving a pearl white Navigator that he was feeling, Paydro was out testing out a navy blue Excursion that he was digging as well, Mookie was out testing out a silver SC400 Lexus coup that he just had to have, and last but not least, Bam-Bam was just now pulling back up into the lot in a black Range Rover, that he was dying to get back to B-More in so that he could get his floss on niggas. They all had their minds made up that they were ready to rule and take over the city of B-More. Black and Bay-Bay walked back to the car lot, all hugged up and lovey duvy up like they were a match made in heaven. As they were walking onto the car lot, Black wasn't looking at his crew; they were getting ready to get their shine on and use the Titanic to shut down every strip that was in a 500 miles radius. Black couldn't wait to form a car line and just ride on through every drug strip and show everyone who's the man for real.

Black said, "So this is how my little niggas living it up for real?"

They all just turned around and said, "Yea this is how real niggas do it when they messing with a real nigga and a true nigga like you Black."

Los said, "Thank you Black for making us who we are, and for helping us to start eating and we are forever grateful and loyal to you Black."

Black said, "All I can tell ya'll is let's get this money."

Bay-Bay said, "I might have some girls for ya'll once we get back to B-More, isn't that right baby."

Black said, "Yea that's true baby."

Bay-Bay said, "Plus with all of the red and white tags floating around, my girls might even give it up messing around with a strong and get money clique or should I say firm like this."

Black said, "I kind of like the sound of that, so there it is ya'll, were the firm, and I said so. So are ya'll ready to rock and roll back to the city?"

Everyone said, "Yea, but let us run over and grab some of that banging chicken."

Cross said, "Yo, Los hit the trunk lever so that I can get the money out for Bobby V."

Cross walked over to Bobby V. and said "Yo, B, its $200,000 dollars in cash in this duffel bag and he threw it to Bobby V."

Cross said, "Yo, B tell Sonny I'll give him a call in a few days."

Sonny is the big fish of the car lot everyone answers to him. Cross really mess with Sonny and they have developed a lot of respect for each other over the past few years. Bobby V. took the bag of money to Sonny and told him it was from Cross and that he was to be expecting a call from him in the next few days. Sonny hung up the phone and he walked out to the lot to send his blessing to Cross. As he walked outside everyone was hopping into their respective cars.

Sonny called Cross and said, "Cross it was nice doing business with you again, he said, Cross since ya'll have bought so many cars today, maybe I'll just give you a call and see how the toys run?"

Cross said, "Sure thing, I'll be waiting for your call and let me know if that count was right in the bag?"

Sonny said, "Will do, and they all drove off heading for the chicken spot."

Everyone ordered the same thing to go, even Black and Bay-Bay ordered some more to take back to eat later on. As everyone was waiting on their orders, Blacks pager went off; it was Dia with #911 in her code. Black walked out of the chicken joint, got into his car and called her right back. Dia answered the phone on the 1st ring crying her little heart out. Black's heart almost stopped just hearing her crying so hard.

Black said, "What wrong with you, is everything okay?"

Dia said, "Don't you baby me right now."

Black said, "What's the attitude for?"

Dia said, "So you just going to outright disrespect me like that?"

Black answered, "What are you talking about now?"

Dia responded by saying," so Black its like that now, when I get knocked up, now you want to be a hoe and start this cheating crap?"

Black said, "girl what are you talking cheating crap?"

Dia said, "Yea, my girlfriends saw you today down on the Avenue all hugged up on some tramp with all of your little fake goons guarding you like your president or the pope, but you know what Mr., it's cool keep right on going you all out in the public eye. Just let me ask you something Black? Why are you doing me like this Black? I thought that you said that you loved me?"

Black said, "I do love you crazy girl, stop tripping about nothing and your girls didn't see me anyway, I'm in V.A. at the car dealership."

Dia said," So what are you doing down there? Oh I see now, I get it, you down there buying your little freak a car. I get it now."

She was crying even harder now and he was feeling so bad for her at this time. He hated making her upset. Black really didn't know what to say to her at this point.

Black said, "Dia do you want me to grab you some of this chicken that you like so much while I'm down here in

V.A?"

Dia said, "No go on ahead and buy your new girl who you was all hugged up on some because I'm not your girl no more, and do yourself a favor and don't even bother coming to look for me and she slammed the phone receiver down into its cradle so hard in his ear that it sent shivers through his ear drum." Black looked at the phone in dis belief, saying to his self I know she didn't just hang this phone up in my ear like that. Black tried to call her right back, but all he kept on getting was a busy signal. He finally gave up trying to call her back, because she was mad and just took the phone off the hook. He went on back into the chicken joint to join back in with everyone else, but he was hot and it showed all over his face too, because as soon as he walked into the chicken joint Cross asked him, "Yo, what up Black. Spill it out to me my nigga?"

Black said, "Yo you're not going to believe that some of Dia's friends drove by us today down on the Ave. while we're all out there giving out the T's and someone called her and told her that they saw me and ya'll but I was all hugged up on some girl."

Cross said, "Word?"

Bay-Bay just stood there not saying a word at all, but deep down inside of her heart she felt that this was going to be the perfect chance for her to move in on her man and help him to forget all about his girl. Black was heated, but Bay-Bay didn't want to add no extra fuel to the fire, so she just kept her thoughts and plans to herself for now.

Black turned to her and said, "Baby girl do you feel like driving back to the city?"

Bay-Bay said, "baby if that is what you want I'll drive back for you daddy."

She leaned over towards him and she kissed him and all he could do was smile at her. Black was thinking to himself, if old girl wants to be tripping like that, then I'm just going to chill out with Bay-Bay for the rest of the night. All eyes were all on Bay-Bay, checking her out from head to toe, she was flawless, drop dead gorgeous and she was looking ever so unique, meaning that she was a very special one of a kind. She was looking just like she had stepped out of the show magazine. She was sexy in her own little way. Everyone's orders were ready and Black paid for the whole entire order. They all grabbed their bags and left out the chicken joint and got into their cars.

Black said, "Yo, we all are rolling in single file lines all the way back to B-More. Bay-Bay going to drive us back and we are going to be riding 3rd place. I know that she will be tired once we get back home and I'll take over and we'll hit up every known area there is and I want to create a little bit of malice. Plus, we have to meet back up with our little clique so we can get the run down and the final results that the Titanic has caused. Let's roll out, and everyone got into their cars."

Cross was first pushing his BMW station wagon, Los drove in 4th pushing his Navigator, Paydro drove in 5th pushing his Excursion, Mookie drove in 6th pushing his Lexus coupe, and last but not least was Bam-Bam sealing off their car show with his Range Rover Truck. All 7 of the vehicles were getting down on I-95 highway, racing back to the city. Black was laid back in his seat feeling real good about how things was slowly but surely changing for the better.

Bay-Bay turned the music down and asked him. "Black you okay, are you mad at me?"

Black said, "Naw, baby girl, why would you think that I'm mad at you?"

Bay-Bay said, "Well for starters because I've caused some friction or should I say unpleasantness in your relationship. If I wasn't out there with ya'll then her friends wouldn't have saw us all hugged up or maybe I should have just stayed my butt in the car somewhere."

Black said, "It is what it is baby, and I'm not mad at you at all, as a matter of fact, can you hang out with me for the rest of the night?"

She was so happy, glad, felt lucky and very fortunate to be the one that was hanging out with Black. She was caught off guard by his question, stunned that he would even ask her a question like that, not a crazy question like that she was thinking to herself. Bay-Bay took a deep breath and answered him.

Bay-Bay said, "Black you know how much I really want to be with you, I'm always at you every beck and call."

Black just smiled at her. Black said, "Once we get to the end of the highway flick your high beams so that they will know to pull over so that we can change up. I'll drive from there that way you can call up your girlfriends to see if they want to hang out with a few players or not."

Bay-Bay just blushed, he always making her blush; they just loved the smoothness of how he talks to them. Black always creates wetness in their panties or their thongs. It's a feeling that girls just can't explain, all they know is that they love the way his presence be making them feel. She told Black that she could handle calling the girls. As he sat and listened to the low music playing he thought about how Dia had hung up that phone on him earlier today. He didn't really know what was up with Dia at this point, but he did know that things were getting ready to seriously change.

CHAPTER 13

Penny called Chrissy's house and she answered on the 4th ring.

Chrissy said, "Hello?"

Penny said, "Girl what took you so long to answer the dag on phone?"

Chrissy answered, "I was in the bathroom, and I didn't hear the phone ringing at first. What's up Ma?"

Penny said, "Girl you won't believe who came over here and chilled with me today?"

Chrissy said, "yea probably daddy."

Penny said, "Nope."

Penny said, "My chocolate King."

Instantly Chrissy knew that it was her brother. Chrissy said, "Oh yea, he finally stopped over there huh?"

Penny said, "Yea and he's probably mad too."

Chrissy asked "mad for what Ma?"

Penny said, "Because I was sitting outside drinking my beer as he was pulling up. Girl I was drunk as a skunk and they fell out laughing at Penny's little drunk joke."

Penny stopped laughing real quick because she knows just how much Black hates it when she drinks.

Penny said, "I can tell you this, we had a nice long talk, you know how my mouth get when I'm drunk. I was telling him about that no good faggot Tony and how he runs his mouth like a little girl. I told him what I been hearing about, how he is always telling their business, and how he just needs to cut that wild coon punk off. I love my son so much and guess what else he's getting ready to do?"

Chrissy said, "come on Ma, I'm tired of the guessing games, just tell me."

Penny said, "he getting ready to bless Mr. Eddie with some back money for all of them times that he use to look out for us when I didn't have all of the rent money or the times when I just didn't have nothing. So Black talking about giving Eddie 21 stacks."

Chrissy just whistled loud on that note, and said for real Ma?"

Penny said, "When is the last time you seen or heard from Lisa?"

Chrissy answered, "Not since the other day when she almost ran into the back of my car. You need to call her and check on her butt for real. You know that she's still a big old kid inside of a grown woman's body, a drunken body at that and they both fell out laughing at the joke."

Then out of nowhere Chrissy turned the table on Penny. Chrissy said, "Yea she gets it from momma and she laughed even harder, but Penny didn't find that little joke too funny at all, but Chrissy was still rolling."

CHAPTER 14

Dia had packed her some clothes and went to her mother's house, because that's where she wanted to be at for a few days. She still couldn't believe that Black had done what he did out in public like that and for him to allow her friends to ride by and catch him. She packed her bags and went and got in her truck, still crying and devastated from what her friends had called and told her, they had witnessed her man doing to some tramp out in the open market area. Dia vowed to herself that she was going to get to the bottom of this mess with Black.

Dia said, "I sure can't wait until I have this baby, so that I'll really have someone who will always love me and care deeply for me. I hate my so-called friends too, because if they really cared for me they wouldn't have told me anything to hurt me or the baby. They know that getting me upset is not good for the baby, so forget those little hussies too."

Dia finally pulled off heading for her mother's house. She called her mother while she was driving.

Mr. Ruby answered on the 3rd ring, "Hello?"

Dia instantly started sobbing a lil harder now, hearing her mother's voice on the other end of the phone.

Dia said," Ma I'm on my way to your house."

Ms. Ruby said, "Girl what's wrong with you, crying and stuff?"

Dia answered, "My girlfriends caught Black down on the

Ave. all hugged up on some tramp, Ma, why does this always have to happen to us good women?"

Ms. Ruby already knew Black had a strong rep in them streets and she also knew that money was power and power runs the world.

Ms. Ruby said, "My child what did I tell you a while ago? I told you remember that you have to let dogs roam the streets for a while, but they will always find their way back home. You need to start acting like a woman, play your position and stop listening to gossip, especially coming from other girls who are probably after your man in the first place. Black never ever disrespected you in your face, does he?"

Dia said, "No not in my face, but I always hear this and that."

Ms. Ruby said, "So what you hear stuff. I hear stuff too, but hearing stuff doesn't buy you trucks, pay the bills, pays for the food, pays for your gas, buy you clothes, pay the mortgage every month, keep your hair done, nails done, toes done, so I suggest you wipe them tears and do you. Plus, which ever one of them girls that called you telling you that mess, if the opportunity presents itself she would most definitely be the first one on her back, legs spread wide open like the red sea, or on all fours doggy style, sucking your man dry, so get yourself together, wipe them tears and keep your head held high and stop all of the stressing so much, it's not good for my grandbaby."

Like I have said to you earlier, Black takes good care of you and he takes care of home, he keeps you sharp, you keep money, ya'll don't have any drama, girl you better keep your #1 and don't sweat the small stuff.

Ms. Ruby said, "If them hoes want to do your dirty work for you and you reap all of the benefits from them dummies sexing him, licking him and sucking him dry, God know whatever else their doing for him and you don't have to do anything and still get wined and dined then let them little hussies do your dirty work for you."

Dia stopped crying and started laughing at her mother lecture, because she knew that her mother was really telling her the truth.

Dia said, "Ma you sure know how and what to say to ease my pain paint the perfect picture."

Ms. Ruby said, "Child I've been there and done that. I've been doing this thing for forever and a day, but I'm okay. He comes home every night and everything is well taken care of, so it's all good by me."

Dia said, "Ma I'll be there in like 20 minutes."

Ms. Ruby said, "Okay then I'll see you when you get here then and they hung up."

Dia was so relieved after talking to her mother. She always was the one woman who knew how to solve just about every problem, there is. Mother's always knows best.

Dia said out loud, "I'm still not going back home. I'm still mad at him."

Dia reached over and turned up her radio and she listened to Alicia Keys' song "Secrets". Just as she was getting relaxed, her cell phone rang and she almost didn't hear it ringing because she was jamming and singing so hard along with Alicia Keys. Dia turned the volume down and answered the phone.

"Ring, Ring, Ring, Hello said Dia?"

Chrissy said, "Dag girl why you let your phone ring that many times?"

Dia said, "Girl I had the radio turned up listening to my jam. Plus, I was singing too, but what's up?"

Chrissy said, "Nothing girl I had just wanted to see what you was doing that's all. I had just called the house and the answering machine picked up, so I just called your phone to check on you.

Dia said, "right now I'm not doing anything, but I'm on my way to my mother's house for a little while, what you up to?"

Chrissy answered, "well I'm not doing anything either,

just got on my mother a little bit earlier."

Dia said, "girl what about?"

Chrissy said, "She called here asking me when it was the last time I seen or heard from Lisa. I told her not since that day you and I was at the market and Lisa had almost crashed into the back of my car. Then she going to tell me that I need to call and check up on her. She also said that Lisa was a big kid inside of a grown woman's body."

Dia broke out laughing hard as ever.

Chrissy said, "Then she said a big drunken body at that."

Then Dia stopped laughing after she heard the part.

Chrissy said, "But guess what?"

Chrissy said, "I said she gets it from her momma, and she wasn't too happy about that."

We just kept on laughing, then we hung up, so I know that my mother was mad at me for that one, but she can't take any jokes that are aimed at her, then she shouldn't dish them out at people."

Dia said, "Yea Chrissy you are absolutely right. A person should only dish out what they can handle, Mrs. Penny is so crazy, I love your Mother to death, and she's always been my girl."

Chrissy said, "Well Dia I was just checking to see what you was doing that's all. How is your pregnancy and prenatal care coming along?"

Dia said," Chrissy everything with me and the baby are fine, but the baby be kicking my butt some nights, and they both had a good laugh."

Chrissy said," Okay then Dia I'll talk to you later on."

Dia said, "Okay then thanks for calling and checking up on me.

Chrissy said, "alright then, and they hung up."

Dia had just now pulled up, parked her truck, grabbed her bags and headed towards her mother's house.

CHAPTER 15

As planned they all came to the end of the highway I-95 and Martin Luther King Blvd, all 7 cars put their hazard lights on and pulled over to the emergency lane side so that Black could switch seats with Bay-Bay and he could take the front lead of the car line. It was now 8:25p.m. Right before Black got into the car everyone had their heads sticking out of their car windows.

Black said, "Yo I have a great plan for us, but I'll tell ya'll about it tonight."
Black said, "Yo Bay-Bay getting ready to line ya'll with."

Everyone beeped their horns to let Black know that they were ready to rock and roll. The very first area that they hit was through Murphy Holmes Projects. They drove through there and all eyes were on the 7 whips coming through with Black in the front bumping that "Me Against the World" 2Pac. Niggas were out there breaking their necks peeping the scenes. After they were done riding through there, they hit up the Dome Boy's area, they hit up the CBS area, they hit up the whole E.A. area all the way up and down, they hit up Mount St., Fulton Ave., Stricker St., Gilmore St., they hit up North Ave., all the way up to Dukeland St., North & P., they hit up R&G, North & Longwood, they hit up every drug infested area and they turned every head in the circumference. Tony was still hanging up on Whitelock St. where it was still jamming at; they were still getting money at this time of the night. Whitelock St. was jammed packed including Tony who was just chilling sitting up on the wall where you can see from every angle of the hood. The firm was most definitely on their way through Whitelock City with the big boss Black leading his goons. They were all shinning like the true stars that they are. Black drove through the slick ways as he came up through the back end to drop in on everyone. He came up Linden Ave. and busted a right hand turn on Lennox St. drove down Lennox St., made a left up Park Ave., made a left on Park Ave., and Reservoir St., came up Reservoir St., busted a right hand turn onto Callow Ave., where it was live and jumping at, everyone was out there looking hard at the firm coming through. Black was definitely sending a big message that, yea we getting Arab money. Some niggas waved and hollered Black, some just started mean mugging. Black went through Callow Ave., passed Newington Ave. and they came to the main focus of where Black hopefully wanted to see Tony at. Black made that left onto Whitelock St. where everyone was out there, including Tony. By this time Black had turned his theme song up a lil louder now and the speakers came to life bumping that 2Pac "Me Against the World", it was thumping loud now and Black was just cruising really slow now. Whitelock St. was his old stomping grounds, so he really wanted to make a big statement on this block alone.

The wall is where everyone hung out at and as soon as Black cruised by the wall he looked and locked eyes with Tony and smiled one of his lil smiles that he always do, to let a nigga know that yea I'm the man for real. Everyone else was waving and hollering Black's name out. Black waved at a few dudes and beeped his horn at a few, but Tony had a look on his face that could kill Black without a gun. Everyone started asking Tony why he wasn't with Black or a part of that long line of big whips that had just rolled through here shinning like new money?"

Tony couldn't speak because he didn't have an answer for that question. He just walked away, mad as ever. Once he saw that, his thoughts went down to his shop and he was wondering what he was going to do if Black shuts everything down on the dope side? He wanted to know how he would be able to sell even 1 pill with Black out on the block taking all of the dope money.

So he started trying to think ahead of Black again. He started trying to analyze a more different approach. Tony thought that if Black takes over the dope game that he had a plan of his own, so he thought. Tony's plan would soon fail just like everything else does when it comes to him trying to out think Black.

Tony said, "Black can have the dope game, I'm just going to start selling all of the coke to go along with Black's bumping dope, yea that's my new plan. I wonder should I run my plan pass Black or not?"

Little did Tony know, Black already had his mind made up weeks ago for his little goons to lock down all ends of this game? Tony was out cold from this blow by Black, he was just still walking round dead in the game. As the firm was still driving around styling and profiling, Bay-Bay asked to use Black's phone so that she could call up to the house where she knew all of the girlfriends would be at. Everyone was always hanging out at Kandace's house out in Aberdeen M.D., that was out in the suburban area and we chilled there.

Kandace had a nice big house out there that was all of our get a way and relax house. Kandace was mixed with Spanish and Chinese. She's a very laid back and simple woman, very driven towards her future goals in life. She just graduated from nursing school; she loves to workout, club every now and then, shop, and just chill out with the rest of the clique. She's 5'9, 143 lbs., really light complexion, she had really long hair that hangs down to her butt, and she's real sexy and catches all eyes. Kandace is a mixture of herself and the R&B singer Amerie, she is bad as hell. Bay-Bay called Kandace house and Jessica answered on the 3rd ring.

Jessica said, "Hello?"

Bay-Bay said, "Girl what are you doing?"

Jessica said," Who is this?"

Bay-Bay said," Oh now you don't know my voice now, this Bea."

Bay-Bay said, "So who is this?"

Jessica said, "Oh Bea, this is Jessica, we not doing nothing, sitting here bored to death, why what are you doing?"

Bay-Bay said, "you wouldn't believe me if I told you girl."

Jessica responded, "I will tell me."

Bay-Bay said, "Girl we just now came back from down V.A."

Jessica said," girl get out of here and why didn't you take us with ya'll? You said we, who is we girl?"

Bay-Bay said, "girl I have been hanging out with the king of the hoods."

Jessica said, "Girl no you didn't?"

Bay-Bay said, "oh yes I did too."

They shared in on a quick laugh and Jessica cut it short with and what was ya'll doing down in V.A?"

Bay-Bay said, "Girl all of his little partners or should I say his peoples' are following behind each other in a single file line of nothing but big boys, you know big whips?"

Jessica said. "Oh girl I need to holla at one of them niggas then."

Bay-Bay said, "They call themselves the firm and you already know that Black is from up on Whitelock St. but everyone else is from around on Gold St."

Jessica said, "Bay-Bay I don't care where they from, I just need me a good man in my life."

Bay-Bay said," Well that's why I was calling ya'll because they trying to hook up with ya'll tonight. Who's all in there?"

Jessica said, "Girl everyone is in attendance, except for you. We all were starting to get worried about you, because nobody has heard or seen you all day long, or you haven't thought to pick up the phone and call to tell anyone that you were okay."

Bay-Bay said, "So Jessica you telling me that it is a full house there?"

Jessica said, "Exactly."

Bay-Bay said, "Dang"

Jessica said, "Dang what?"

Bay-Bay said, "There's not enough of Blacks people for all of ya'll hootchie mammas, I guess they will just have to choose for themselves who they like then."

Jessica said," I guess they will then, so when do we get to meet these fine gentlemen?"

Bay-Bay said, "hold on for a minute girl, she reached over and turned the music down a little bit so that Jessica could hear her ask Black, so Boo where are we headed to right now, because I have got in touch with all of my girlfriends."

Black cleared his throat and put on his deep sexy voice. Its 9:42p.m. And you know that we have to go to that meeting at 10:00p.m. that I had set up with my peoples from earlier today, so how about we hit them right back as soon as the meeting is over with and adjourned with."

Bay-Bay said that sounds like a plan to me, she turned the music back up and resumed the phone conversation that she was having with Jessica."

Jessica said," Girl does he look as good as he sounds?"

Bay-Bay said, "Girl yes in deedy and they share a little laugh.   Well they have a meeting to go to at 10:00p.m. tonight and I guess they will have to call back once their all done okay?"

Jessica said, "Alright then girl, but wait, so do I suppose to tell everyone else or not?"

Bay-Bay said, "Yea go ahead and tell all of them that I got some real dudes that's trying to holla."

Jessica said, "Okay, then we'll be waiting for you to call us back and they hung up the phone."

After Jessica had hung up the phone with Bay-Bay, she ran into the room with a crystal glass and a spoon and she stood in the middle of the room and began to clank the glass with the spoon to get everyone's attention. Everyone came into the room, cut the music down because I've just received some good news from Bay-Bay.

Jessica said, "She's alright and she said that she loves all of us."

Everyone breathed a sigh of relief hearing that their friend was okay.

Jessica said, "Bay-Bay said, she's getting ready to come here in a little while, she's been down in V.A. all day long, while we were worried sick about her butt. She was having a lot of fun and just chilling. Does anyone have a clue as to who's she's been chilling with?" Jessica looked around the room to see if anyone would raise their hand to guess, but everyone had a puzzled look on their faces as if she had just asked them a bewildering or perplexing question.

Jessica just yelled it out, "She's been chilling with Black all day long ya'll!!"

Everyone in the room had a stunned look on their faces as if they were knocked senseless, then Nicole asked Jessica, "you talking about the king Black?"

Jessica answered, "Yup that will be the one."

Everyone in the room broke out laughing because they knew that if Bay-Bay got Black, his crew was most definitely on the hit list next for them.

Jessica said, "Bay-Bay and them are on their way out here to meet us, she said they had to go to a meeting or something and they would be out here, the guys wants to choose some of us, the bad part about it or the bad news is that its only like 6 of them coming out here tonight."

After she told them that it was only 6 guys coming out there tonight, everyone got up and started getting their swagger together. They all wanted to look their best for when the firm arrived at the house. A lot of the girls ran to go and jump into the shower, some were doing their hair, doing their nails, they all were pampering themselves, getting ready for a showdown tonight. Black led the way to the meeting, but he made it his business to drive through Bloom

St. It looked just like a ghost town. Tony's workers weren't working at all they was hoping to see Black so that they could apologize for using the name of his dope, but they were sure to make it very clear that Tony made them do it. They were very sure to tell Black how Tony was beating people up because they didn't want to cop from him and they only wanted to buy Titanic.

So they were forced to do it or get beat up pretty bad. Black and his crew drove around the corner to Gold St. where this meeting was getting ready to take place at. Black parked the car and told Bay-Bay to get into the driver's seat and that he would be right back in a few minutes. She got out and walked around to the driver's side, got in and she locked the doors. She reached back and grabbed her food and started eating some of her chicken. Everyone met the workers at the very same place that they gave the testers out at. Everyone was prompt and showed up just like Black had asked.

Black said, "Okay everyone listen up, as he was getting ready to discuss the details of their meeting he was interrupted by Tony's workers. Two of the women who Black had hired to work when him and Tony was partners were crying and Black couldn't understand what Tony's workers were still doing outside at this time of the night and or why these 2 women were standing here crying their poor little hearts out like this. So the hitter of Tony's crew stepped up and told Black what all had taken place right before he left earlier today.

The hitter said, "Black you know I'm only here because you're the man who put me on right."

Black shook his head and said, "Yea I know that, but what's the problem here?"

The hitter said, "We had come out today right after ya'll gave out them testers. It was so slow out there for Dot after what ya'll had done at 3:00p.m. With the testers. People were still buzzing around asking for the Titanic dope. It was so slow Black that we were stuck on 1 bundle for like 3 hours.

Tony came to ask me how many pills did I sell and I told him 3 in the last 2 hours. It was so slow that Dot couldn't make $100.00 dollars, and when we use to be with you we was always rolling. We'd at least make like $4500.00 dollars every hour or so. Black I'm going to keep it real, today I think we made at least $25,000.00 or $35,000.00 thousand dollars in less than 4 hours.

Black stood there puzzled at what the hitter for Tony had just told him, but he let dude finish telling his story as everyone else listened to him too.

The hitter said, "Black today Tony lost it he was beating people up, hurting people and physically abusing people because they didn't want to cop his dope. He then turned to all of us and made us act and lie to the people and tell them that we had your Titanic dope."

Black was steaming after just hearing that Tony was using his name and disrespecting him for the very last time.

The hitter said, "Black we had no choice or he would have did something to us as well."

Black said, "So Tony wants to play dirty huh, Ya'll go on ahead as if ya'll have never ever had this conversation with me, I'll look into trying to get all of ya'll a spot on the Titanic team. Keep on doing what ya'll doing. Make sure that ya'll keep me posted."

They all thanked Black.

Black said, "ya'll two better cut all of the crying out, talking to the women who he had hired when him and Tony was together."

They both was sniffing a little bit because Tony's whole crew knew that they were wrong for using Black's name on that dope for Tony but that they had no choice in the matter. Black could have had something done to all of them, but he gave them all passes. They thanked Black for not being mad at them and the whole Dot crew left Black's crew and the meeting continued as planned.

Black was in heavy thoughts while they were on the highway heading to take out the rest of their crew. He just couldn't get this coke idea out of his mind. So he just started adding and putting his plan into motion.

Black said, "I'll have to cop like 30 kilos of cocaine to take to the streets in the same hole as my dope. That way people can kill 2 birds with 1 stone. Get their dope and coke all in one motion. Let me see, split 2 ways, 36 O's at $2,000.00 dollars off of each joint will be $72,000.00 dollars, each worker gets half each time we run a brick through the hole. I'll always make real sure that my crew is straight no matter what, but we will have to split the pay for the coke and whoever runs the coke will make out as well. I'll use Tony's crew to push the coke. Back to the meeting at hand."

Black said, "Alright then before we got off the track."

Los said, "You were telling everyone to listen up."

Black said, "Okay then listen up. We're a team and we must work as a strong team. Everyone will get money on our team, that's my word. I will always play fair with everyone that's on my team. All I ask is that how I treat you, you treat me. Now ya'll know that we have the best dope in the city right now and I'm going to do everything in my power to keep it like that. My corner people please keep your eyes open, no slip ups, no missed calls, guard this team as if your life depends on it, and to be very honest with you, it does. I'm giving all of you a raise starting tomorrow, all of the corner people which, it's like how many Cross?"

Cross said, "Its 6 corner people in all."

Black said, "Each corner person will be making $250.00 dollars a day from now on and we have how many on the pay roll? Each gunman will make $350.00 dollars a day and I take it that we have 1 hitter and 1 collecting the money right?"

Cross said, "Yup."

Black said, "They will make $400.00 dollars a day. Does anyone have any questions?"

Everyone agreed that they were all making good money. They really did appreciate Black's kindness; they already knew that they could never ever make nowhere near the type of money that Black was paying out with no other crews, so everyone was all good with Black.

Black said, "Now the Titanic is getting ready to sink every dope shop around here under the water, plus we also will have coke running out of the same hole on opposite sides. It's going to be really going down. I've learned an old saying from the first man to give me my very first pack. So I'm going to repeat it to ya'll, like it was told to me. Ya'll can take it for what it's worth, but yea I learned the hard way so, ya'll take heed. Dude told me to put some money up for those rainy days that are ahead of us, we can't see into the future so be prepared for what you can't see."

Los said, "So what color tops we using for the coke then?"

Black said, "I guess we'll use red tops for the coke. So I guess it will be Titanic and Big Red's. There it is then."

Everyone clapped their hands because it was now or never, come up sink.

Black said, "So in a few days we'll have two more new people added to our team who will be running the coke through, everyone will have a chance to meet them as well. Well that's all I have for ya'll at this time, everyone be good, get some rest and we'll see everyone out her at 2:00p.m. sharp tomorrow and everyone make real sure that you give Cross your whole entire name and info, so that if need be we'll be able to bail ya'll right out of jail, if in case anyone gets bagged for anything, and the workers all left."

Black and the goons walked over to Black's car. He looked at his new girl Bay-Bay, and she was just chilling doing exactly what all girls do, talk on the phone and gossip, gossip and more gossip. Black winked at her and she waved at him. Black turned around to face everyone.

Black said, "Yo, ya'll don't even trip, were going to act as if we don't even know what Tony did today, but he'll pay in due time, mark my words. Anyway let me just run this pass ya'll so that we'll have an understanding of the plan. Ya'll are my guys and nobody is bigger than the next man and with that said, this is what's going to happen. Its 6 of ya'll right?"

Cross said, "Yes."

Black said, "So once we get the coke jumping each of ya'll will take turns running the bricks through the hole. I figured it out already, we will make $2,000.00 dollars or $1,800.00 dollars off of each ounce right, times 36 ounces, that's in each brick and that's a total of $72,000.00 dollars off of each brick, now with that ya'll just keep on stacking up ya'll's money. We'll keep track of the order and whose run it is. Whoever turn it is gets done will take $30,000,00 dollars for the people's who's running the coke shop, and that means I'll get $30,000.00 dollars also its another $12,000.00 dollars to pay people who's working the coke. Is that fair enough with ya'll?"

Cross said, "Yea Black that's all love right there."

Black said, "Now this extra coke money is just that, extra, it doesn't have anything to do with ya'll pay concerning the dope. Plus, I will come up with a nice phat raise for ya'll as well, as soon as we get this thing on lock and key which won't be that long at all, but ya'll keep on stacking. Ya'll have new whips now, how ya'll like them things."

Everyone told Black that they felt like they were on cloud 9.

Black said, "I have a surprise for ya'll. Bay-Bay called up her friends and it's a full house of all kinds of girls. She said, that ya'll will have to pick for yourself who you want to holla at and who you like and all of that good stuff. I'm booked for the night. I'm staying at the hotel with Bay-Bay tonight. So are ya'll ready to roll out?"

Bam-Bam said, "So Black so where do these girls live at?"

Black said, "Yo they out there in Aberdeen M.D. I think her name is Kandace."

Day-Day said, "Yo that's out in the suburbs isn't it?"

Black responded, "Ya'll crazy and started shaking his head at Day-Day."

Cross said, "Yo we better go on and fill up our tanks before we head out there then, because I would really hate to run out of gas on the highway."

Black said, "Yo lets rock and roll then."

Black got into the car and told Bay-Bay to go to the gas station right there on North Ave. across from the car wash. She drove right to the Crown gas station and everyone filled their tanks and they hit the highway with everyone following right behind Bay-Bay.

Bay-Bay said, "called this number for me please, 410)666-2323 and the phone rang 2 times before Kandace answered it in her sexiest voice."

Kandace, "Hello?"

Black said, "Can I speak to Kandace?"

Kandace said, "This is me."

Black passed Bay-Bay the phone.

Bay-Bay said "Hello?'

Kandace said, "Hello, hello?"

Bay-Bay said, "Hey girl, were on our way out there so you'll better be ready."

Kandace said, "Okay then we are ready and they hung up."

Kandace got up and went right to tell everyone to be ready because they were on their way. Bay-Bay just called me and told me that.

Bay-Bay said, "I need to hear me some Keyshia Cole, do you mind Black?"

Black said, "Naw go ahead and do you, and he laid his seat back and closed his eyes as Keyshia's song came to life "Heaven Sent".

Bay-Bay interrupted his thoughts and said, "So, Mr. Chocolate, what's going to happen to us after tonight?"

Black opened his eyes and asked her what do you mean by that?"

Bay-Bay said, "Well you know how it is after us women allow a dude to get into out thongs, they act like we don't exist anymore, so what should I expect from us?"

Black said, "Bay-Bay you already know that I'm really digging you and you know that I had Dia way before you, plus you know how this crap goes, but you also know that me and her are on rocky soil, so your still going to be mines."

Bay-Bay just shook her head, yea, plus she has always loved and respected Black, because he always kept it real and he never lied to her or tried to play games with her, so she didn't have any choice but to love and respect his gangster.

Bay-Bay said, "I don't mind being 2nd and I'm going to be doing everything in my power to win your heart and may the best woman win your heart Black."

She leaned over real quick and kissed him real soft. She told Black that she been feeling, and digging him from the very first time that she laid eyes on him. With that being said, that's why can't none of these wild coon niggas out here say that they had me because I've always considered myself your girl and I've always belonged to you. Black was at a loss for words on that note. All he could do was smile at her. Everyone else's minds were on the very exact thing. All of the 6 of them was thinking to their self, man I sure hope these girls are no birds or chicken heads, or mud ducks. Los also was thinking about how he was getting ready to blow up like the ramen noddle soup, inside of some 180-degree hot water. He was just laughing and bumping 2Pac's Mackavelli C.D.

Los said, "All I need now is a bad girl to call my own."

Los is 24 yrs. old, 5'6, 180 lbs., light skin, wavy hair, 2 golds on his fangs, light brown eyes, very handsome, nice body, and he stay in the gym every chance that he gets, plus he's ripped up, got ab's like finger waves, he's a very fly dude, real laid back, He's a real suave and polished guy. A real ladies man and polite, and he's just searching for the right woman.

Cross is 6'2. 195lbs, dezel, 22 yrs. old, brown skin, brown eyes, he wears corn rolls and all of the women be dying to braid his hair. Very good looking, medium build, dress nice, stay fly.

Paydro is 25 yrs. old, he's an ex-boxer champ, in perfect shape, nice 8 pack abs, 6'1, 205lbs, he's a fair looking guy, always looks mean low haircut, temple taper, he has tats everywhere.

Day-Day is 5'6, 140 lbs., 23 yrs. old, has curly hair, he's into boxing on Sunday's that's his workout, real quiet, only speaks when spoke to and he likes to dance.

Mookie is 26 yrs. old, 5'10, 170 lbs., real dark skin, black like tar, has gold up top and his bottom of his mouth, very confident man, outgoing, plays a lot of basketball, he plays in the summer league over East Baltimore at the Dome.

Bam-Bam, he's 21 yrs. old, 5'7, 135 lbs., he's a school boy, just coming off of the steps getting money. He's just like Black use to be, hungry to get that money, so Black pulled him in like Apple Sider gave him a run, As the 7 cars were getting closer to Kandace's house Bay-Bay called the house and Lizz answered the phone.

Lizz said, "Hello?"

Bay-Bay said, "Who is this?"

Lizz told her "This is Lizz, Bay-Bay".

Bay- Bay said, "We're getting ready to pull up Lizz, so tell everyone that I said we are here and they hung up."

Black said, "Dang baby, with all them girlfriends you got, it's going to be hard for them guys to choose someone huh?"

Bay-Bay said, "It's like 42 girls that hang out together and their from all over the world."

Black said "Oh yea that's what's up."

Bay-Bay said, "Black I'm going to say this to you once, please don't every disrespect me and cross the line and mess with one of my friends, because things can get pretty ugly."

Black said, "No need in you making all these threats, you got that baby."

The firm had finally made it to Kandace's house. When they pulled up in front of the house Kandace was sitting on her porch with Jessica. When the cars finally came to a stop, both the girls stood up and was waving to Bay-Bay as she was getting out of Black's car smiling and waving back at them. Black got out of the car and just stood there against the car as the rest of the clique walked up and stood facing the house.

One by one each girl came outside and they all stood in a single file line just as Bay-Bay had told them too, each girl walked down and over to the clique. They all stood in front of them and said, her name, age, height, weight, measurements, sign, and whatever else they wanted to say, where they were from and smiled at the firm clique. The first girl that came strutting down was Bay-Bay to show all of the girls their example of how she wanted this thing to be done. She walked down in front of the guys.

Bay-Bay said, "Hello, my name is Bay-Bay, I'm 27 yrs. old, 5'7 150 lbs., 36-24-40, I'm a cancer and I'm from B-More, she also stated very loud and clear, that I'm already spoken for, my man is Black, she winked her eye at him and walked away to join the rest of the girls."

While she was walking away Los turned to Black and told him that Bay-Bay was gone off of him."

Black just smiled and said, "I don't see it."

Bam-Bam said, "My nigga she's most definitely wifey material."

Black said, "who are ya'll telling, but ya'll know that Dia be bugging and will try to kill one of us and they all started busting out laughing."

Kandace came walking down looking as sexy as she could be, stopped in front of them and said, "Hello my name is Kandace, this is my house, I'm 23 yrs. old, 5'9, 143 lbs., 36-27-39 I'm a Virgo, I'm from Boston, she winked her eye at them, licked her lips, and she walked on back to where the others were at. Bootie shaking like jello as she walked back.

The firm took notice immediately at her performance; Kandace had every tongue hanging even Black's.

Day-Day said, "Man shorty was like a 10."

Christina walked down next, she said, "Hi, I'm 26 yrs. old, 5'8, 148 lbs., 36-26-39, I'm a Leo, I'm from Delaware," and she walked off, then came another girl, my name is Melyssa, I'm 29 yrs. old, 5'8, 150lbs, 34c-27-38, and I'm a Taurus, I'm from Philly and she walked off."

Leana said, "Hi, I'm 30 yrs. old, 5'11, 156 lbs., 38-24-42,

I'm a Pieces, and I'm from Buffalo, and then another one came down, hi my name is Kim, "I'm from New York, I'm a Aquarius, 25yrs old, 5'7, 135lbs, 38-26-42, hi my name is Tyra, I'm a Virgo and I'm from B-More, I'm 19 yrs. old,6'0, 162lbs, 36-34-38, I'm Libra and I'm from B-More, My name is Mia, I'm 27 yrs. old, 5'8, 153 lbs., 35-28-38, I'm a Cancer."

Gabrielle said, "Hi I'm 23 yrs. old, 5'8, 148lbs, 34d-24-36, I'm a Aries and I'm from L.A., I'm Reagan, I'm 22 yrs. old, 5'6, 138 lbs., 34c-25-37, I'm a Capricorn, and I'm from Chicago, my name is Trina, I'm 24yrs old, 5'7, 152 lbs., 36-34-33, I'm a Scorpio born in Japan, but now I live in Alabama, My name is Kia, I'm from Canada, but now live in New York, my name is Lauren, I'm 29yrs old, 5'11 156lbs, 38dd-36-42, I'm a Scorpio born in Germany, but now live in California, my name is Angel, I'm 27yrs old, 5'2, 136lbs, 34c-33-38, I'm a Leo born in Australia, but live in D.C. and right after she said that she was from D.C., Black stepped up and told everyone that it was getting late, plus they seen enough of them fine sisters to last them a lifetime, but we think that the clique can pick from what they have seen thus far.

Black said, "Whoever doesn't get picked tonight, don't trip, I have more people that ya'll can holla at. I won't let ya'll down."

As the picking was getting ready to begin, Bay-Bay walked over and stood in front of Black with her butt resting up against his wood. He held her around her waist which was so small. The first to choose his girl was Los.

Los said, "I want shorty right there, the one who's house this is."

Kandace just broke out smiling because she was the first one to get picked. She walked down to Los, hugged him and he hugged her back and whispered in her ear, my name is Los and you're the most beautiful woman that I've ever had in my life. Next to pick was Cross, and he called for the shorty with the red pants on, referring to Angel, she walked down to Cross kissed him on his cheek and she thanked him for picking her. Cross said, "Baby girl I would have hated to see you with someone else other than me."

Next to pick was Paydro, I like the shorty right there wearing the pink sundress, asking for Stacey who was looking stunning as ever and she walked over and jumped into his arms hugging and holding him tight around his neck. Paydro said, "Girl you smell so good and I could really get use to this kind of affection."

Stacey said, "Yea I could too. "

Next to pick was Day-Day, "let me holla at shorty right there pointed at Gabrielle. She put her hands up over her mouth and asked Day-Day who me? He shook his head yea and she walked over to him with tears of joy in her yes, he embraced her. The next to choose his girl was Mookie, but he didn't call her to him, he decided that he was going to walk over there to her. He walked over to where she was already standing at. Mookie just had to add his own swagger to this; once they were staring into each other's eyes they both spoke at the same time.

Mookie said, "My name is, and she said, my name is."

Mookie said, "Go ahead, ladies are first."

Leona said, "My name is Leona:"

Mookie said, "hi Leona I'm Mookie."

Next up was Bam-Bam, I like short with the 2-piece skirt on, shoes hot, and Melyssa stepped forward and walked down to Bam-Bam and gave him a nice big hug and kiss.

Melyssa said, "Hi."

Bam-Bam said, "Hi I'm digging you."

After Bam-Bam chose up on Melyssa the show came to a complete halt. Black then cleared his throat to get everyone's attention.

Black said, "the rest of you fine sisters remember that I got ya'll in a few days, Bay-Bay will keep all of ya'll posted. We have big day coming up in a few hours so we have to get going, like I said I got ya'll."

Black hopped into his car and Bay-Bay waved bye to the

rest of the girls and she got into the car, the rest of the clique walked to their car as well. They all held onto each of their girl's hands. They got into their cars, wrote down each other's number and any other contact info. Everyone kissed their new girls, said their good nights and the firm rolled out as quickly as they came. They left leaving a fleet of nothing but bad chicks in a daze waving them off. All of the girls who got chose tonight were very happy, but at the very same time, sad for the ones who didn't get picked. It was back to business as usual. It was now 12:15a.m. And Black's pager went off, he peeped at it and it was Dia, but he didn't call her back. He noticed that she wasn't at home and that she was at Mrs. Ruby's house still mad, so he was spending the rest of this morning with is girl Bay-Bay.

Black chirped everyone's phone and let them know that he was headed to the Ritz hotel downtown and that he would hit them all up later in the morning, everyone hit back and told Black that they got where he was going to be at, and they all went their separate ways. Black and Bay-Bay checked into their room. Black's eyes were roaming all up and down her entire body. All Black could think about was licking and sucking Bay-Bay's big titties, and his wood instantly got hard as a brick. She wanted him so bad. Black walked over to her and reached up to massage both of her titties right through her blouse. She gasped for air and began licking her lips, pulling him towards her and began to kiss and lock her lips onto his, her tongue just probing into his receptive mouth hungrily. He began to allow his hands to roam all over her, up and down her soft body, cupping her phat butt cheeks and pushing his wood against her throbbing coochie. She was moaning so many different languages, moaning and calling his name over and over. He began to undress her, lifting her into his arms and carried her to his making love, awaiting king size bed where he lowered her. She had started to kiss and nibble on his ears, kissing his lips, cheeks, and sucking on his neck as he moved real swift. Black hungrily took her titties into his mouth. He gently sucked and bit each nipple as she felt nothing but pure sensation, she was over excited. Each and every time that she moaned, she was telling him just how good it felt to her and that she was soaking wet, dripping her cum juices all over the sheets. She went from moaning into little light screams of passion.

Bay-Bay said, "Ohh, ohhh, ohhh, yes Black."

He felt her legs quiver; they were shaking and trembling so bad, that he was getting ready to stop and she begged him to put his wood inside of her. She grabbed his wood and started stroking it gently. He was still sucking on her nipples as she guided him right down between her legs. She was so hot and wet that he could feel her heat and radiation as he inserted his middle finger inside of her super wet, sloppy and drenched wet coochie. He worked his finger back and forth, side to side and up against her clit with his thumb causing a lot of friction and an ill feeling that sent her over the edge as the movements and heat intensified, had Bay-Bay going crazy, calling his name, begging him to never stop.

Bay-Bay said, "Black I'm cumin, I'm cumming Black, don't stop, please don't stop."

She was moaning and shaking like she was having involuntary contractions of her leg muscles and coochie muscles.

Bay-Bay said, "Black this feels so fantastic, so extraordinary, so unusual and very exceptional. I love you Black."

He raised up so that he could get a better look at her facial expression, her body wetness, the sweat shimmering, glistening, glittering, sparkling, and shinning from her sweat and the light from the full moon. Bay-Bay made Blacks breath get caught up in his throat, just seeing how sexy and beautiful she really was. Her coochie was really pretty; shaved so nice and wet you could see it running out of her.

He cupped her titties again, sucked them some more, just a little harder then he did before, which caused her to squirm with more pleasure and desire. He used his thumb and forefinger and he squeezed her nipples hard and harder until she cried out softly.

Bay-Bay said, "Black I want you, please take me, I really need to feel you inside of me, put it in me, give it to me Daddy."

He kissed her softly and whispered to her Bay-Bay there's no need to rush and he went down below. He traced his tongue down her flat stomach, down to her wetness, kissed her coochie lips, sucked her clit, which drove her into a shaking fit. She was trying to squirm away from the hold that he had on her. She was moaning and screaming his name, then he slid his tongue inside of her, deep inside of her wetness, hitting spots with tongue that she never even knew existed inside of her. He worked his tongue so good that she had cum like 5 times back to back, screaming his name.

Bay-Bay said, "Oh God, yes, yes, yes go faster Black, go faster."

Black obliged and he speeded his rhythm up and she clamped her legs on both sides of his head, holding his head in place so that he could swirl his tongue deeper into her wetness sending her into la la land. He grabbed her butt cheeks tightly and just grinded his mouth inside of her, he felt her trying to squirm back away from him again, shaking and screaming.

Bay-Bay said, "I love you Black."

He was drenched with sweat; her body was craving and crying out in sexual urgency.

Bay-Bay said, "Black please put it back in me."

Black took his sweet time, Black was taking her to a place a new height that she's never ever knew existed. He wanted her to always and forever remember who took her to places that she'll never in her life forget. This was a night

Bay-Bay would remember for the rest of her life. She was going wild, he grabbed his wood and rubbed it up and down over her wetness, her clit and she wheezing, trying to catch her breath, making so much noise, and her coochie was pulsating, throbbing and quivering. She was begging and screaming for him to put it in and the time had come for him to finally enter into her coochie, he couldn't prolong any longer. He gripped the sides of her hips, tensed up his stomach and legs, took his right hand and inserted his wood into her, all of the way until their stomachs touched her inner walls close around his wood and she fit him like a glove, a tight fitted baseball glove.

Bay-Bay was nice and tight. He just pushed and stayed real still for what seemed like an eternity as he looked her in the eyes and she stared at him in his eyes and told him that she loved him so much. He started to slow down his pace, moving in and out, nice and slow. Black began to move in slow circular motions, round and round, digging deep into her essence, her being as a woman, their sweat mixing with each other's, the smell of their love making essential scent that smelled like good sex between the two of them. Her juices were lubricating to his wood with every stroke that he took inside of her, which made him really slippery. She kept on moaning, grabbing his face, pulling his ears down to her, whispering sweet I love you to him, planting kisses on his lips, neck and anywhere she could. He was really enjoying himself. His girl or his old girl Dia was far away from his mind. He now was starting to feel that tingling sensation, letting him know that his nut was on the way. He grabbed her titties, her eyes were shut tightly, her breathing began to pick up, and she was now breathing out of her nose and her mouth. He began to pound her hard and faster. At this time, they both were telling each other that they loved each other. She was screaming, telling him don't stop. He was gritting his teeth, staring at her sexy, and sweaty face as he kept on pounding her back out for all that this love making was worth.

Bay-Bay wrapped her legs around his waist and she matched him thrust for thrust, giving it all to him. Black's wood was starting to get that twitching feeling, and he told her that he was getting ready to bust a nut. Black looked her in her eyes, half closing his eyes, toes started to curl up, his grip on her legs was much tighter as he asked her to cum with him as he shot his load up inside of her. As she was taking him to another world, to ecstasy as rapture feeling as she cried out with him that she was cumming also. They both was nutting at the very same time, she was digging her finger nails into his back and screaming.

Bay-Bay said, "oh God, Black I'm cumming."

While they came together Black had speeded his stroke up which was causing friction again, creating the spot that he was hitting to make her keep on cumming, simultaneously, everything he was laying on her created so many different feelings that were occurring all at the very same time. Bay-Bay was hooked, he had whipped her now. She's not whipped by herself; they both were on the very same wave length. They both had worn each other out; they held onto each other and kissed until they dozed off into la la land. Black hadn't made love or slept this good in a very long time, plus he was definitely feeling Bay-Bay. She didn't have no man except for this new found relationship that she now has with him and he wanted to keep it like this as well.

CHAPTER 16

Black and Bay-Bay had awakened up real late into the afternoon. They had indeed satisfied each other last night, they slept really well. Their love making was so intense, so very strong, sensitive, eager, and vivid, she was so sore due to her lack of intercourse, mutual dealings or any kind of sex or connection with a man in a very long time. She was so pure and sacred. She was very dedicated to herself and vowed that sex was just so over rated, but with Black things was different. She felt as though she was a born again virgin, but she told herself that she could really get use to making love to Black every night, at least she thought that she could. They woke up and kissed and Bay-Bay went on into the bathroom to take a shower and brush her teeth and get ready to start her day.

While she was in the bathroom getting herself together, Black grabbed his phone and pager and noticed that he had missed a lot of calls on both his phone and pager and he just smiled, thought to himself that the reason he missed those calls was really worth every missed call. He went onto chirp every one of his partners, they all answered and let him know that they were all good and that everyone was sitting at the I- Hop eating breakfast, discussing everything that took place down in V.A. the meeting, and the Rip the Bay-Bay way. Black just laughed and told them to chill out and that he would hit them right back in a New York second. Before they disconnected Cross wanted to know "Yo Black, so what was she like?"

Black said, "Yo, she mean with it."

Cross said, "alright then my nigga, we'll see you in a little while then, and they hung up."

Apple Sider had finally sold everything and he couldn't wait to see Black and show him that he's right back on top of his game. Thanks to him for putting Apple back on top of his game plan.

As Apple was riding around, he decides to hit Black up and see what was good. Black's phone rang 5 times and Bay-Bay answered it.

Bay-Bay said in her sexiest voice that she could muster up.

"Hello, whose calling?"

Apple Sider pulled the phone away from his ear and stared at the phone like the phone was speaking to him or something, then he pressed the phone back to his ear while Bay-Bay was asking him are you there."

Apple Sider said, "Yea I'm here, may I speak to Black?"

Bay-Bay said, "He's in the shower, who should I tell him is calling?"

Apple Sider said, "Tell him it's Apple Sider."

Bay-Bay said, "Hold on for a minute please and she went into the bathroom and sat down on the toilet while he was washing up."

Bay-Bay said, "I answered your phone for you and you have a call from Apple Sider. What do you want me to tell him?"

Black said, "Who is it again? I have soap in my ears and it's hard for me to hear you.

Bay-Bay said, "It's Apple Sider, what you want me to tell him?"

Black said, "Oh Bay-Bay tell him I said to shoot through Gold St. at 2:30p.m. today and I have something that I want to show him, thank you Bay-Bay."

Bay-Bay said, "Hello"

Apple said, "Hey I'm here."

Bay-Bay said, "Apple he said to shoot through Gold St. today at 2:30p.m. And they hung up."

Bay-Bay said, "Black I told him what you said and he said that he would be there. Black can I ask you a question?"

Black thought for a quick second, what it is, and said you ask me."

Bay-Bay said, "Is that the Apple Sider that had fell off of his high horse."

Black said, "Yea that's him, that's my main man, and the last I heard he's back on top again."

Bay-Bay said, "The last time that I saw him he was looking really bad, people was joking all on him and everything."

Black said, "Oh yea, well you know that everyone that go up must come down and everyone that go down must come back up. The rule to it all is that you just don't ever stay down, get right back up and you try it again, next time even harder. He was the very person that taught me about the rainy days that's always ahead of us. He's the very person to ever lend me a helping hand when nobody else would."

Bay-Bay said, "Are we even talking about the very same Apple Sider?"

Black said, yea we are, Apple Sider is a real friend of mines."

Bay-Bay just broke out laughing at what she was hearing. Black said, "I bet you a dollar to a doughnut that my man Apple Sider is back on his feet again."

Bay-Bay just walked away shaking her head because she knew and she could remember very clearly that the last time she saw Apple Sider, he was so busted up, she thought that he had started getting high, just like all of the rest of the dudes do. Bay-Bay just didn't have a clue as to just how strong Apple Sider truly is. Apple drove straight to his block to see if his little man and the rest of the clique were all the way done or not. When he pulled up, his block was jumping off the hook. Apple had made his mark once before, so it wasn't never ever really hard for him to get back on top again. He just needed a plug to do it with. Now he has a good, hungry, go hard team that's all about their money. He put his little team together. His man Marlo, had a few little niggas who was starving to get on, so they took Lexington St.

& Monroe St. they had things on lock and key down there, Apple pulled up on the block in his black on black 745 BMW. His whole clique was like; Yo Apple we see you doing it real big again.

Marlo said, "Apple I'm really proud of my nigga, its real good to see the old Apple Sider I once knew back on top again."

His whole entire crew was admiring their boss's new car.

World said, "Yo Apple that joint mean my nigga."

Apple Sider said, "Yo in due time ya'll will be coping some new joints as well, so don't even trip, and as matter of fact on our next run ya'll got whips coming, everyone."

They all gave each other high fives, yea now that's what's up.

Apple said, "Yo Marlo take a little walk with me, so I can holla at you real quick."

They both walked and hopped into Apples' car, Marlo let the window down and told the rest of the crew that he would be right back and Apple pulled off, and parked a little ways up the block.

Apple said, "Yo how much do you have left?"

Marlo answered, "We only got like 10 g packs for the rest of the day and were on hold."

Apple said, "Don't even trip, did you ever get to go and count that money up from the other day?"

Marlo said, "Yea, I counted it up and its $120,000.00 dollars in cash. I put it up inside of the red box, plus that last bundle of money too. I think that's like $40,000.00 dollars, plus we got $10,000.00 dollars and 10 g packs left. I talked to everyone and they all agreed to be down for the cause, they know that were in grind mode, plus things have really picked up for us for real. I mean real good."

Apple said, "Yo it's not funny, but other niggas getting ready to have some big problems out of us and I love it."

Marlo said, "Yo, I have been hitting the rest of the crew off with a few dollars, just a few hundred that's all, plus the corner people's hitters and everyone is on the same page. Everything is operating really smooth for us right now."

Apple said, "Marlo you just don't even know that we're getting ready to really blow up, you ready my nigga?"

Marlo said, "You already know that I'm game. I've been dying to get a break like this, plus the rest of the crew, yo they are hungry too."

Apple said, "Yo, listen to me nigga, I got all of ya'll, plus I'm playing fair with each and every last one of ya'll."

Marlo said, "Well let's go ahead and shoot to Pa Pa's house and pick that money up."

Apple said, "I have to go and meet the connect at 2:30p.m. And when I get back we're going to blow this area into our own little city."

Apple pulled around to Pa Pa's house and Marlo got out of the car and went to his stash in Pa Pa's house, got all of the money, put it all into a footlocker bag and went to get back into the car.

As Apple pulled off Marlo, said, "Yo its $170,000.00 dollars in cash in the bag, and don't forget we still have the 10 G packs left."

Apple dropped Marlo back off on the block. Marlo got out of the car and told Apple peace and drive safe. He shut the door and joined the rest of the crew. Right before he pulled off, Apple rolled down the car window on the passenger side and said, "Yo I don't see any of ya'll with them new Jordan's on yet, what part of the game is that?"

Everyone just stared at Apple for a minute, and then they all looked at each other, then at their feet.

Apple said, "Yo Marlo, close up right now and ya'll cop them new J's. Use some of that pack money, get fresh for today."

Once everyone has showered and got themselves right, chirp one another and then ya'll can open shop back up, around 5:00p.m. Finish up the last packs for today. Every one of them was smiling like crazy. They were smiling so hard that their smiles were up to their hairlines.

Apple said, "Yo, Marlo tell the workers that they are on hold for about an hour too. Give them all 2 pills too. Marlo I'll see you in a little while and he drove off to meet up with Black."

Everyone spoke at the same time; yo that car is off the chain.

Black got dressed and was on his way out to take Bay-Bay home and his pager went off. It was his old partner Tony. Black just shook his head, and then he was just wondering what was dude paging him for? Black called him right back and Tony answered on the 2nd ring. "Hello?"

Black said, "Yo you paged me?"

Tony said, "Yea, Yo where you at?"

Black said, "Why what's up?"

Tony said, "Aint nothing up, but I wanted to run something by you, it's a great idea too."

Black responded by saying "Well if it is that important then shoot through Gold St. at 3:00p.m., I'll be down there."

Tony said," okay then yo, I'll be there and they hung up."

Bay-Bay said, "I don't like him that nigga Tony is no good baby and Black just smiled at her. I been paying close attention to ya'll and he's not hanging around you like ya'll use to be, so I guess you cut that snake off huh?"

Black said, "You know what Bay-Bay?"

She said "What Black?"

Black answered, "I'm never one to cut people off, I let them hang and cut themselves off."

Bay-Bay said, "Well Mr. Black Face, I really enjoyed myself last night, it was really nice being with you. And you know what Black?"

Black said, "What it do Bay-Bay?"

Bay-Bay said, "You was as good as I dreamed that you would be baby, and much, much much more Mr., you also put a hurting on my kitty cat for real and she leaned over and kissed him and asked him did you like it?"

Black said, "I loved every second of it, now that's what I call making love. I sure wouldn't mind getting a double dose of you girl, like every night and day, and they both smiled at one another."

Bay-Bay stopped smiling and got real serious and told him this coochie is all yours for the taken, while you're laughing. She said "I know already that you have a girl, but Black I'm in love with you too, and I want to be your girl as well. I just know that your other girl will slip up and make a mistake, and guess what?"

Black asked, "What?"

Bay-Bay said, "I'll be right there to fill in where she doesn't."

Black pulled up in front of Bay-Bay's house, and right before she got out of the car she leaned over and kissed him so soft, smooth and passionately that the kiss mesmerized him, leaving him speechless. She reached over, opened the door and walked on into the house. Black waited until she went in the house and closed the door then he pulled off. As he pulled off his mind was on his other man who had played a major role in who he had become today.

Black called Boo-Boo's phone and he answered it on the 4th ring, "Hello?"

Black hit him with, "what it do my Nigga?"

Boo-Boo said, "Yo, Black I was just sitting here wondering what you were up to out there in them streets?"

Black said, "Yo what it do my nigga?"

Boo-Boo said, "Yo we need to talk as soon as you can make a little bit of time for a nigga like me?"

Black said, "Yo is it serious?"

Boo-Boo said, "Yea, yo, it's that serious and it concerns your dude T-Mac. Yo, I got lucky and ran into him the other day. Yo word up, your man has changed up his whole swagger, his looks, his walk, and he even dress funny now."

Black said, "So how is he Yo?"

Boo-Boo said, "He's okay as long as he just keeps it moving. He's pushing a rental car now. He told me that he chilling out is the only way that he will be able to get by at this present time. I need to sit down with you Black and run this puzzle by you as soon as possible. So Black when do you want to me to breeze through and check you out?"

Black said, "Well I have to meet up with all of my people at 3:00p.m. Today, so shoot through there then I'll be out on Gold St.

Boo-Boo said, "Alright then my nigga, I'll be there and then hung up."

CHAPTER 17

Dia called Black's phone and he answered on the 1st ring,
Black thought that it was Boo-Boo calling him right back, so he answered his phone.

Black said, "Yo what did you forget to tell me now?"

Dia said, "Well first of all I didn't forget to tell you anything, she told him."

Black said, "Oh what's up, I thought that you was Boo-Boo calling me right back because we had just now hung up."

Dia said, "Black what's going with you, and why haven't you called me all day? You probably were all shacked up with that lil tramp you was with the other day. So now you don't care about me no more or it even being still an us?"

Black said, "Dia listen to me, I'm a very, very busy man, and I don't have a second to waste on arguing, and playing no kind of little games, and no he said / she said games okay. I'm a grown man Dia. Those so-called friends or little girls of yours are the same little freaks who are trying to holla at me on the low and you mean to tell me that you're just going to jump the gun and run crying to Mrs. Ruby like the world is coming to an end. So you stayed over there all night long huh?"

Dia said, "Yea I didn't want to be around you, you hugging all up on some little tramp, then trying to come around me, hugging all up on me and my baby like you haven't been around no one else."

Black said, "Now see I just told you that I don't have time for arguing and Black hung up the phone right in her ear."

Dia was really mad at the news that she had received from her girlfriends and now Black had just hung up in her ear to add insult to injury. Since she's been carrying the baby she hasn't been up Whitelock St. where the little kid Jim be at with Sampson and the rest of the dudes from up on Whitelock St. Dia hasn't been being a faithful little woman as everyone thought her to be, she's been freaking and pulling a few little tricks of her own when her so-called man Black isn't available, or of use at times. The lil dude Jim is nobody she went from greatness to real dirty, busted, non-beneficial, nor profitable, and always causing trouble. Black hates the lil kid Jim was a passion. He always felt that Jim wanted his girl, plus Black and the kid stayed into it, fighting for no reasons, but it was obvious to Black when he use to hang up on Whitelock St., but he never had any solid proof.

He really couldn't put his finger on it, but word kept on circulating around that his girl Dia and Jim was messing around on the low, low. Black felt it all in his heart. He really did love Dia to death and right before she got pregnant she had already crossed Black for another dude names, Posey, back in the days, right before Black had blew up, Posey and Dia had started messing around real tough but her heart and mind stayed on Black while her physical body was with the dude Posey. It was definitely true Posey had her but not her heart. One day the dude Posey had received a lil settlement out of court for a sum of $90,000.00 dollars. Dia was right there to be a part of the settlement money, but what she did not know was that Black's money was still stacking up while the lil money that Posey received from the car accident was steady getting low, and was running low fast. Dia and Posey kept on spending and Black kept on stacking. Dia and the man that had her body kept on spending the money like it was going out of style.

Until one day she just decided that she really wasn't happy and that she was growing tired of sneaking behind Posey's' back to creep with the real man that she really loved and cared so deeply for. Dia decided that she wanted to break her relationship off. She decided that she wanted to be back with Black.

Every day, she started staying far away from Posey, stopped answering all of his calls. She had finally made up her mind that she really wanted to be with Black and one day word was going around that Dia was creeping and was seen on many different occasions with Black. Posey was hearing it buzzing around as well, but he didn't have any proof of the affair until one day he was walking and Dia and Black was just chilling hugged up. He saw Dia and Black with his own eyes this time around standing there right before his eyes, he was heated. Posey didn't know what to do, so all he could say to her was that he didn't want to be with her no more, and that their relationship was over with.

While he was telling her that it was over, it was already over with a long time ago when she made up her mind that she wanted to be with Black.

Dia said," it's over now you know that Black?"

Posey had already heard how she was going around Black's mother's house every day, sexing Black like crazy. Dia didn't even want to see Posey again; she was truly done with him. Little did she know she would never ever again possess Black's heart fully? When she started messing around with Posey, Black was scarred and he started knocking girls every day all day.

Dia had created a monster inside of Black, that no woman in the world would ever be able to trick him into being with them every again. Black had so many girls and it was all because of Dia, and her wanting to be freaking with niggas like Jim and Posey. Black and Dia got back together, at least she thought that she was his main girl again, he had so many girls. Black had expanded the whole city on all sides of B-More. Black still went to pick Dia up every day and every night to stay with him, but the other girls was definitely getting their fair shares of his time and sex as well. He was digging Dia's back out a lot. That's how she became pregnant with lil Cliff. She had started to calm down a little bit, but lil Jim stayed up in her face. She always had to deny that she was messing around with Jim, but Black felt it in his spirit that she was.

Dia had finally had little Cliff and Black was right there as his first seed came into this world out of her womb. Once little Cliff came out the doctors' wiped the baby body off, wrapped him after Black had cut the umbilical cord to separate the baby and Dia. Black walked off to the other side of the room while the doctors; worked on Dia to put her stitches in to close her womb back up. Black was so happy when his son came out into the world. Black eye's filled with so much hate and for all of the pain and hurt that she had caused for him in the past by being a little under cover freak while he stayed true to her, he never looked at another girl, Black was faithful as a pair of water proof boots and they keep a person's feet from ever getting wet in the rain, but once Dia crossed him he never ever forgave her or maybe he did forgive her, but he just would never ever forget it. Black vowed to himself that he would always have a lot of girls on his team.

Dia was definitely one girl that was out of the question for him forever. As time went on Black kept on hearing all kinds of different stuff about what Dia was doing or messing with this dude or that dude. Lil Cliff was growing up and Black kept the baby and Dia with him a lot now. He kept on blowing her back out, but she was just his baby mother now. That was her title, not his girl, because he has a fleet of girls on his team now. Lil Cliff had just turned 1-year-old. And

Dia pops up pregnant again. Black was hearing everything, all types of stuff and all kinds of different rumors, unproven statements, hearsay and it was just common talk about the 2nd baby not being his child, but Black doesn't pay what the streets are saying no mind. All he does is confronts Dia about what he's been hearing all around town about her 2nd baby not being his child.

Dia said, "Black shut boy, this is your baby, and all of them people are messing with your head, they are hating Black, you know that everyone hating on our relationship."

Black is feeling all of the pressure that's on his shoulders, he doesn't go around her as much as he use to. Black is really upset with Dia for being a freak, a no good trick.

Black said, "Dia you should have never cheated."

That image of her sexing someone else and someone stretching his girl open plays over in Black's mind. All he could do or say to her is that she brought everything on herself. Black closed his eyes and thought real hard. In his mind all he could come up with is that he had to get a blood test with the 2nd baby.

Dia started crying and asked, "What you have to get a blood test for Black? I know and you know that this is your baby. I know because I have not been with anyone else but you Black."

She use to always win Black over with all of her crying and pleading her case. Black would then fall for it and they would push all of the rumors to the back of their minds, but as always the hearsay would always start right back up again. Black would pull all the way back up off of Dia. She would page him and ask if he would go with her to the doctor's appointments, but Black never ever went with her with the 2nd baby. Black started hearing so many new dudes' names floating around that his baby mother was supposed to be messing around with. A dude named Saul, Jim, Posey, Little, Woodrow, and Pooh.

After all of those different names started surfacing he knew Dia wasn't any more good. Dia had finally had the 2nd baby and she paged Black over and over, so that he could be at the hospital when the baby was coming out of her, but he never called her back. He had his mind made up that the 2nd baby wasn't his. Black finally called her back, hours later, after she had the baby already.

Dia said, "Black why you not here with me while I'm having your 2nd baby Black?"

Black said, "Dia listen, I'll be down there in a little while and he hung up on her."

Black finally showed up at the hospital,

Black said, "Excuse me Miss Can you tell me where Dia's room is please?"

The nurse pointed to room #225. He walked into the room; she was holding the new baby as he slept in her arms. There was a knock on the door and another nurse stuck her head in the room.

The nurse said, "Excuse me Sir, are you the father of the baby, because visiting hours are now over with and you will need to wear this band in order to stay in the hospital."

Black said, Naw, I'm the father, I was just checking in on her, I'm getting ready to leave now."

Black walked over to the bed to get a closer look at the baby. The baby didn't look like little Cliff at all or he didn't favor Black. Black vowed that he would get a blood test to make sure that what Dia is claiming about the child being his was true or not. As time kept on passing by, Black started to accept the lil baby as being his own, do to the fact that it wasn't no other dude coming around to see the little baby. Black was in deep thought as he thought of how trifling and dirty of a woman Dia is. Black had a good heart and children are just so innocent. Black kept on hearing the he said, she said, rumors all day every day.

CHAPTER 18

Black snapped back to reality, knowing that he had a few meetings at 3:00p.m. Plus they were giving out more testers, seeing Tony, and Boo-Boo.

Black said, "Dag I almost forgot about Apple Sider Too."

Black called up Cross, and he answered the phone on the 2nd ring.

Cross said, "Hello?"

Black said, "Yo, what's the word?"

Cross said, "Yo it's almost show time, and your man Tony just drove by here looking like he was searching for someone."

Black said, "Yea, dude said that he got something to talk to me about. I'm not even sure yet what he wants, but I'll be there in a little bit, it's like 2:40p.m. right now. Is everything set up?"

Cross answered" yea, you know its jammed pack out this joint again."

Black said, "Oh word, that's what's up."

Black was just getting ready to park his car when his phone rang; he answered it on the 3rd ring. Black said, "What it do?"

Bay-Bay said, "I just called you to tell you that I love you Black that's all."

Black said, "I love you to Bay-Bay, what are you doing?"

Bay-Bay said, "Nothing, I just got out of the shower."

Black said okay then I'll see you in a little bit then."

Bay-Bay said, "alright then you be safe out there baby alright."

Black said, "Okay then I will baby."

Bay-Bay said, "Here catch this,"

Black said, "Catch what?"

Bay-Bay said, "This big kiss that I'm sending you through the phone right now and she kisses through the phone."

Black said, "I got it baby, and here is one back for you too, and Black blew her a kiss back through the phones, and they hung up."

He parked around the corner, He said to himself, man it's a whole lot of people out this joint, and Cross wasn't lying. All of these people we should clear $100,000.00 dollars easy today."

It's now 3:00p.m. And Black had been awaiting this day, seems like forever and a day, but its going down now. As Black was walking down the street he noticed a black on black 745 BMW just cruising pass, he thought that he recognized the driver of the car but the dude had on a fitted cap with it pulled all the way down to his eyes like he was hiding, but Black had to give the dude his props. The joint was nice and clean. He looked up and spotted Tony parking his car. He looked up again and the 745 BMW was riding back in his direction again, but this time Apple Sider was facing Black and they both made eye contact. Black was so happy to see that Apple had bounced back just like he had done years ago when he only had $250.00 dollars left to his name. Black was smiling and yelling.

Black said, "Ooh my man back on now, my nigga back on."

Black was really proud and happy for Apple Sider. Apple pulled up beside Black before Tony could reach him.

Apple Sider said, "Yo, Black hop in."

Black hopped into the car and they drove off.

Black said, "Yo, this joint is hot to death my nigga, when did you get this joint."

Apple Sider said, "I had this joint for a few days now, naw I meant to say a few weeks now, but I have to give you something my nigga."

Black said, "What is it?"

Apple Sider said, "I know that you are very busy and all of that good stuff, I can see all of these people out here waiting on you. Where did you park at?"

Black said, "I parked right around the corner."

Apple said, "lets shoot to your car real quick."

Tony had just missed Black as he saw him hop into the car with Apple. As they drove pass, Tony threw his hands up into the air to ask Black what was up."

Black rolled down the window and said, "Yo, I'll be right back, wait right here for me."

Apple Sider pulled off.

Apple said, "Yo, Black grab that bag that's on the back seat."

Black grabbed the bag and Apple thanked him.

Apple Sider said, "Yo, you saved a nigga from sinking for real. Its $170,000.00 dollars in that bag."

Black looked at the bag, then at Apple and whistled.

Black said, "Yo, you pumping hard aren't you my nigga. They reminisced on their old times laughing and joking around.

Black turned serious and said" Yo do you need something else?"

Apple Sider turned around looking Black straight in his eyes and said, yea, my nigga I need a whole brick of that raw dope. I need to do it real big now, shut everything down around my way."

Black looked at Apple and just smiled.

Apple Sider said, "Yo Black why you looking at me like that?"

Black said, "Why I'm looking at you like what?"

Apple said, "Like when you first came on my block letting me know that you were really ready to get that paper, you had this little smirk on your face and your still doing it right now."

Black replied, "Yo, I can do that for you that's not a problem, but I have a lot to do right now. Where are you headed to right now?"

Apple said, "I'm waiting on you."

Black said, "Alright then, let me put this money in my trunk so that we can go around here and give out these testers and open up shop."

Black got out of the car and put the bag of money in the trunk of his car and hopped back into Apples car and they drove off heading back to his block.

Black said," Yo, this joint rides nice and its real quiet. I like this joint yo, it's good to see you back on top again."

Black said, "this time around I'll give you the greatest lecture that was ever told to me."

Apple Sider said, "Let me hear it then."

Black said, "You told me this a long time ago. Make sure that you put something away for them rainy days that are going to hit."

They both looked at each other this look that said we've both felt the wrath of not practicing what we preach, and not doing the things that we are taught. They learned a very valuable lesson the very hard way.

Apple said, "Yo, Black I won't take your words to me lightly, I'll take them kindly and I will wrap them around my neck this time around. Out of the $170,000.00 dollars, only $120.000.00 dollars is mines. I put your $20,000.00 dollars plus only $30,000.00 dollars to pay for the 200 grams that you gave to me, so $50,000.00 dollars is yours off the top Black. So if it's cool I'll owe you $30,000.00 dollars and I really do appreciate you and everything that you've done for me.

Black said, "Yo, I'll call you as soon as I get done with

taking care of this business on the block."

They shook hands and Black shut the car door and Apple pulled off staring at Tony as he was checking out his car. Cross walked over to where Black and Tony were standing at.

Cross said, "Yo, Black here we go. The next thing you heard was Titanic "T's in the hole, its so many people out there it was crazy "T's in the hole, Titanic, Titanic in the hole."

All you hear is screaming and everyone running for that Titanic dope. Tony was at a loss for words. He just looked hard at all of these people ripping and running for the Titanic. He also thought about what he did the other day, when he was acting all disrespectful towards Black, by using his name to sell his packs.

Tony was really trying to come up with a way to tell Black what he did, but he first wanted to run his plan past him first to see if he could get on. Bam-Bam peeped a stick up boy on the move as if he was trying to bring the firm a sneaky move or something. Dude appeared to have not noticed that he had someone who was watching out for stuff like this. Bam-Bam definitely wanted to send a message to everyone, whoever wanted to try some grimy stunts like this.

The stick up boy was working alone on this day and he was headed right to the front of the line where the hitter was passing out the pills at. Bam-Bam was hot on his trail with his .44 desert eagle in his hand, already cocked. Bam-Bam didn't really want to jump the gun without a cause, so he waited to see just how things would play out. The stick up boy didn't even have a clue that this was going to be his very last and final time to ever try another stick up move like this ever again. As the hitter was passing out the last few pills he had, the stick up boy was pulling out his gun, getting ready to rob the hitter, closing in on him, when Bam-Bam came out of nowhere and unloaded his whole clip into the stick up boy's body. He shot him 2 times in the head at close range which sent brains and half of the stick up boy's skull flying everywhere.

He was dead before he even hit the ground, he didn't have a chance with Bam-Bam on him. He had holes in him the size of golf balls. Bam-Bam fired the rest of the shots into his lower body. People were scared to death, just at the sound of the eagle, put fear in people. It sounded like someone was shooting off a cannonball out there. The sound of his gun sent people rushing like a stampede, like a herd of cattle, but it was a crowd of people running for their lives. Everyone was frightened. After today there will not be any more games or trickery being played with the Titanic boys, Bam-Bam has just set the stage... Tony was scared to death when he heard those gun shots ringing out. After the shots, people were still trying to cop the Titanic, but it was getting ready to get hot as fire cracker around there. You could hear the police sirens from a distance.

Cross backed tracked where the shooting took place at and he picked up the .38 revolver that the stick up boy had dropped onto the ground. Cross sent word to move the shop around the play ground near Chocolate City. That's where we're going to be sending everyone to if they still want to cop Titanic. It was still a big ole crowd of people out there waiting to get their dope, even though the stick up boy just got bodied. Police was everywhere swarming all around. As everyone was headed towards the playground.

Black turned around and asked Tony what he wanted to holla at him about?"

Tony said, "Yo, since you got the dope on lock and key. I'm wondering if I can run some coke with your dope in the same hole?"

Black just busted out laughing at Tony's comment.

Tony said, "Yo what did I say that was so dag on funny?"

Black said, "Naw, it is funny that you asked me that, because I already brought some bricks of coke to run with my dope already. I'm going to let my team run the coke so naw Yo, I can't save you my nigga."

Tony was heated and he looked so sad, but it wasn't funny at all.

Black said, 'Yo, so how is business for you down on Bloom St.?"

Tony said, "Truth, it is a ghost town around there."

Black said, "oh yea my nigga, I heard that the other day you was using my name and telling people that you had the Titanic. What's up with that my nigga? You just going to disrespect me like that? Plus, people been telling me that you were actually beating people up, kicking and putting your hands on people. Yo, you can't do it like that my nigga."

Tony said, "Yea, you right yo, I was way out of line for my actions and I truly apologize to you."

Black just stared at Tony and asked him.

Black said, "Yo, why you hate me so much?"

Tony looked away and said, "I don't hate you Black, you're my man."

Black then said, "You know what Tony, you're the bottom of the crab barrel," and Black began to walk away.

Tony said, "Yo, Black?"

Black turned around and said, "Yo, Tony we use to be jumping back on that block, $50 to $60 g's a day, what happened?"

Tony said, "Black I lost focus for real, I've been kind of stressed out here lately."

Black said, "Tony first of all you have to learn how to remove your pride problems, be yourself. It's always cool not to know everything and it's always good to have people around you who know a little bit more then you do, it's okay to fall or fail, just don't stay in that same state of mind, you fall down, get back up, dust yourself off and try it all over again. You know something else Tony?"

Tony said "What?"

Black said, "If you were better than me in anyway or in anything, I would tip my hat to you, and do everything that I could to become like you or even better in whatever it is that I'm lacking in. I would learn from you, take notes, and better myself as a man. Yo, you're not even close to me Tony. Do you have any clue how to play chess?"

Tony said, "No, I've seen different people playing it, but I don't know how to play it."

Black said, "I can tell you don't know how to play the game, because rather if you want to accept this or not, I'm a true king and the people that I surround myself with, I want them to grow and become kings as well, but it's a lot of people who are nothing but pawns. You have proved yourself to me that you're indeed a true pawn Tony. Pawns are nothing, but you have to keep your eyes on the pawns because at times pawns can cause a lot of trouble and Tony your fake, you cause a lot of trouble. You try to play the 50 and I've done nothing but been good to you and fair to you ever since we met. Why do you have so many problems with me, why you want to walk in another man's shoes?"

Tony said, "I don't have anything against you."

Tony was talking to Black but he couldn't look him in his eyes while he was talking to him.

Black said," why you want my shine Yo?"

Tony said, "Black I don't want your shine."

Black took off his shoes, and kicked the shoes towards Tony. Black said, "Yo, do you really think that you can fit these right here pointing to his shoes. Tony do you really think that you can stand the test of time? Can you even fit my shoes, Yo, Tony would you ever cross me? Black just shot question after question at Tony."

Black waited on his answers. Tony just stood there looking all crazy, stuffing his hands in and out of his pockets, but he didn't have any answer to any of Black's questions.

Black said, "Yo, Tony when you can answer my 3 questions then you holla at me. He told Tony peace and he walked away leaving him looking silly as ever."

As Black walked away he noticed that Gold St. had 5-0 out there everywhere. The hole that they used to give out the testers in had yellow tape, crime scene tape was everywhere, police was swarming the hole and as he walked a little bit closer, Black saw a dude laid out dead as a door knob, blood was running out of him everywhere. Even the white sheet that the police used to cover his body with was soaking wet with blood.

Blacks' anger had shot to the roof. He was pissed off that it was a dead man lying in his place of business. Black didn't know what had just transpired at this time, but he does remember hearing gun shots while he was talking to Tony, but he didn't pay the shots no mind at the time.

About 5 minutes later Boo-Boo walked up to Black and asked him what had happened to Yo that was lying on the ground dead?

Black said, "I don't know but whatever had happened, it's getting ready to be hot as a fire cracker out here today. Yo, Boo-Boo what's up with my man T-Mac?"

Boo-Boo said, "Come Yo, let's take a lil stroll and they walked towards Black's car and they hopped in."

As soon as Boo-Boo was getting ready to start telling Black about T-Mac, his phone started ringing. Black answered it on the 2nd ring, what it do?"

Cross said, "Yo, where are you at?"

Black said, "I'm still down the street."

Cross said, "Yo, we are hitting up on Chocolate City now."

Black said, "Oh word, up on the playground."

Cross said, "Yo, hitting around C-City."

Black said, "I'll shoot through there in a minute."

Cross said, "Okay then, I'll see you when you get up here and they hung up."

Boo-Boo said, "Yo, I saw T-Mac and he told me that the fed's were all over him and that he's been hitting and missing. He sent word to tell you to slow down because there up on Whitelock St. also. He told me that he hopes you're not a target up there as well." Black sat there listening to Boo-Boo talk, but his mind was racing now.

Black said, "T-Mac said, that the feds are on me?"

Boo-Boo said," Chill out Black, he don't know it for sure, but you just have to be careful out here. You already know that you're the man out here, at least for down here where your shop is Gold St. belongs to you and the rest of your clique. You and your people's have one edge on everyone else, ya'll have one good and positive thing in ya'll's favor, its keeping ya'll safe at this present time. Black do you have a clue as to what I'm talking about?"

Black said, "I think that I do, but tell me?"

Boo-Boo said, "What's keeping you and your whole team safe is that ya'll don't be doing no type of violence or stupid murders. You know that these people will allow you to get all of the money that you want to get, but once all of that shooting, killings, and bodies start popping up, there coming to get ya'll."

Black said, "Yo, do you still have that one dude number who be hooking up them scanners and putting them trackers on them?"

Boo-Boo said, "You know what? I'm going to have to give that nigga a call and grab some of them scanners so that we can listen in on them people's like they are listening in on us?"

Boo-Boo said, "Yea, then we all follow them clowns around all day like they be following us around too. I'll take care of this as soon as possible."

Black said, "Yo, Boo-Boo stuff is so weird right now."

Boo-Boo said, "What's up yo, talk to me."

Black said, "Man my shorty have a lot of bad and I mean super bad, drop dead gorgeous girl friends who wants me to hook them up with a few of my partners."

Boo-Boo said, "Oh word."

Black said, "I'm not lying Boo-Boo you trying to holla at one of them?"

Before he could even answer, Black told him these

shorties's are fine as hell.

Black said, "My girl Bay-Bay got friends that are out of this world. My whole clique just picked like 6 of her girls last night. Yo, Boo it was a show that was out of this world. I mean it was so crazy how beautiful these women were. I had to cut it short. I was harder than an aluminum baseball bat. Yo, I just couldn't take it any longer. I had to roll out. It was like 40 something shorty's all hanging out at one house. They were all lined up on the girl's front yard like they were in the Miss America's beauty pageant or some kind of dramatic show or something. They called it the Rip the Bay-Bay's run way. I was laughing but it was all the way true, no doubt about it."

Boo-Boo said, "Okay you've convinced me, count me in."

Black said, "I have a plan set in motion already with how I'm going to do everything."

Boo-Boo said, "So tell me how you are going to do it then?"

Black said, "I'm going to rent us one of those big tour bus joints and bring the girls up Whitelock St. so that Sampson and Chuck and all of the rest of their teams can pick them a shorty as well."

Boo-Boo said, "Yea Yo, that's most definitely a good look."

Black said, "I'll be sure to keep you posted, now where are you posted at?"

Boo-Boo said, "I'm parked around the corner on Division St. right on the corner of Pressman St."

Before Boo-Boo got out of the car, Black asked him, "Yo, Boo, do you need anything?"

Boo-Boo said, "not really, but if you come across some bricks of coke give me a holla, because I have a little something in the mix."

Black said, "Yo, I'll give you a call in the morning because I got some bricks of coke on the way."

Boo-Boo said, "Yo, Black is there anything that you can't

get your hands on?"

Black just smiled at Boo, and said, "I'll call you, and Boo shut the car door and Black pulled off."

He was now headed to the playground to see what Cross and the rest of the clique was up to. As soon as he pulled up he could see was that it was flooded, people was ripping and running around every which way, copping that Titanic. Money was definitely being made despite the murder that had taken place earlier on around on Gold. St. Titanic wasn't even out for 1 hour yet and they had sold 10g packs already, because business was on point. Black walked over to Cross, and they shook hands.

Cross said, "What's up Yo?"

Black said, "Nothing much, where is everyone else at?"

Cross said, "Yo, man Bam-Bam just bodied the stick up kid that was laying on the ground in our hole."

Black said, "Oh word, yea the dude tried to make a move on us like that?"

Cross said, "Yea, Bam let the nigga have everything that he had in that cannon."

Black said, "He did it with that eagle?"

Cross said, "Yea, and he had holes in his dome the size of golf balls."

They both fell out laughing.

Black said, "Yo, I'm getting ready to cop everyone a scanner from the nigga Mark in the morning."

Cross said, "Oh word?"

Black said, "Yea word is out that them big boys are starting an investigation up on Whitelock St. and supposedly around our area. Plus, I've heard that they were already on T-Mac. Now this stick up boy just got his cradled knocked back, so that will most definitely add some extra eyes around here as well."

Black chirped Bam-Bam who answered right back. Black said, "Yo, what it do my nigga? Yo, you good?" Bam-Bam said, "Yea I'm good, Black I didn't have a choice, but I'm chilling. How are things around there?"

Black said, "Everything was real smooth around the way, but that it was crazy hot out here, hot as a fire cracker."

Bam-Bam said," Yo, I'm at the movies, but if you need us we'll shoot back through right now."

Black said, "Naw, were good around here, ya'll just lay low and be easy. Yo, call that lil shorty up that you knocked last night. She was nice too."

Bam-Bam said, "Yea that would be good look. Maybe I'll call her and see if she'll come and chill with me or not?"

Black said, "Yea you go on and handle that my nigga." Bam-Bam said" just maybe we could pull off a double date thing, me, you, Bay-Bay, and ole girl?"

Black said, Yo, I would do that but you know that I have so much on my plate right now. I'll take a rain check, but you go on ahead and do your thing. I'll holla at you a lil bit later on and they hung up."

Black said, "Yo, Cross you not even going to believe what that nigga Tony had the nerve to ask me?"

Cross said, "Yo, I can't even begin to even imagine, that dude is a wild coon for real. What did he ask you Yo?

Cross said, "Can he get in good graces? Or can you be his man again?"

Black said, "You're very close, but he asked me if he could run some coke through the same hole that were running the dope through since I got the dope on lock and key."

Cross fell out laughing when Black told him what Tony asked him.

Cross said, "You got to be joking right?"

Black said, "Naw Yo, I'm dead serious, and I laughed in that niggas face."

Cross said, "oh word, that's bugged out."

Black said, "Yo, to be honest I don't really know what kind of time this nigga on, but he's really lost his mind. That nigga is very lucky that I have not killed his butt yet. He's lucky I'm still allowing him to breathe some of this fresh air in."

Cross said, "oh so now you playing God?"

Black said, "Naw, I can never ever compare to God, but I tell you this, I'm the closest thing to God in the flesh that he'll ever get to see."

Cross said, "Yo is it cool to be hitting around here?"

Black said, "Yea this is all a part of our area, we're good around here. I have a funny feeling that nigga been putting salt on me with everyone that's up on Whitelock St. as well. I just can't seem to be able to connect all of the dots yet, but in due time the puzzle will unfold. Yo, I've lived up on Whitelock St. all of my life and for all those niggas to just up and be hating on me like that, it's something that's causing them to have this kind of hate towards me. I'll be having the tour real soon and I guess once I bring them girls through, I'll talk to the heads of the clique's then. I can't wait to see just what that snake Tony has been up too. I can feel it my nigga."

Cross said, "Yo, Black chill out man. Don't let that nigga get you off of your hook up. You have to stay focus on the good things. You always tell us that everything that's done in the dark will always be brought into the light. So we'll get to see what we need to see, just chill."

Black said, "I'll holla at you in a little while. I have a few things that I have to tie up. They shook hands and as he walked away Black said, Cross don't forget to tell the hitters not to forget to let everyone know that we'll have them red tops of fish scale coke soon. I'm going to go and holla at dude in a few, so you be safe out here. Oh yea, how did you like that girl you knocked last night?"

Cross said, "Man I owe Bay-Bay big time for that hook up. She plugged a nigga in real good, plus that was the best lil show that I've seen in a very long time."

Black said, "yea, I liked how she did that lil joint up, run way huh."

Cross said, "Yea, that was off the chain for real."

Black said, "Alright then Cross, I'll holla at you in a lil while and Black walked off to his car."

CHAPTER 19

Chrissy answered the phone after 4 rings, "Hello?"

Black said, "What it do lil sis?"

Chrissy said, "Nothing, where are you at?"

Black said, "I'm on my way over to your house right now."

Chrissy said, "Oh yea, what is it doing, snowing outside and they both started laughing, because it was a surprise to hear Black tell her that he was on his way to her house."

Black said, "Girl you're a trip, big head, and it's not snowing at all, as a matter of fact it's really nice out here for real. I just wanted to stop by to holla at my lil sis, that's real talk."

Chrissy said, "Well I'll just see you when you get here then" and they hung up.

Black got into his car and pulls off. He was driving for only 8 blocks and the police car came out of nowhere and jumped right behind him. He played it cool, but he was kind of nervous due to the fact that he knew that he had almost $200,000.00 dollars in cash in his trunk. He came to a stop light and the police car was still right behind him. The light turned green and Black kept on driving. The police car kept on trailing behind him for blocks, so Black played it cool and just pulled into the McDonalds and grabbed something to eat. He drove right to the drive thru intercom and the police car kept right on going about its business. He sat in the car and found out that what had just happened was really kind of strange. Talking to himself, he said, "I wonder why they didn't pull me over? He didn't have any answer so he just ordered his food and right before he had finished ordering his food, he called Chrissy and asked her did she want anything to eat while he was at Mickey D's?"

Chrissy said, "Yea grab me a #2 value meal with a milk shake."

Black said, "I got you, I'll be there in a few and they hung up."

Black paid for their orders and rolled out. When he pulled up Chrissy was already sitting outside on her front porch waiting for him to pull up. As he was parking, she came down to the car to greet Black with a nice hug. She hadn't seen him in a while. As she came up to the car he rolled down the passenger side window and told her that he was getting ready to pop the trunk and for her to grab the bag of money and go put it up for him. Black hit the trunk lever it unlocked and Chrissy walked to the trunk and grabbed the bag of money and they went into the house.

Chrissy said, "So I see the wind blew you through here huh?"

Black said, "Naw I was just thinking about you that's all. Where are the children at?"

Chrissy said, "Mommy came over here and they wanted to go with her, so she gave me a lil break."

Black sat down to get ready to eat, but before Chrissy sat down she told him that she was going to go upstairs and put the money up for him real quick, and Black take this bag is kind of heavy too. How much is in here anyway?"

Black said, "Like $170,000.00 dollars ", she told him, dag my big brother is rich. She ran upstairs to put the bag up, washed her hands and came right back down stairs to eat real quick. When she came back he was just hanging up his phone.

Chrissy said, "Who was that?"

Black said, "It was nobody, I just paged my dude and put your number in, so he's going to call me back on your phone."

They were sitting there eating and talking, and just like clockwork 10 minutes later Chrissy's phone started ringing. Black answered it with food all stuffed into his mouth. "Hello?"

Black said, "What's up my friend?"

The Connect said, "How are you at the happenings?"

Black said, "I need to have a nice sit down with you, if you're not too busy?"

The Connect said, "Everything is clear on my end."

Black said, "what time and where at?"

The Connect answered," at 7:00p.m. At the ESPN Zone down town."

Black said, "Okay then my friend, and they hung up."

Black turned around to Chrissy and said, I hate Dia so much."

Chrissy said," And why is that Black?"

Black said, "Only if you knew what I'm going through with that trick. She be creeping around with that little dirty nigga Jim and your so right she's cool as a person, but you know just being in a relationship it just was different."

Chrissy said, "Yea you right, I really can't speak on that right there, but I use to always be hearing she wasn't right in that area of her life, but if I was her I wouldn't ever go under you , it would have to be someone who's doing way better then you and its so very hard to compare another nigga to you Black, that's why I'm happy that you are my brother and not no dude that I'm trying to get with, I just know that you're not sweating over no Dia anyway all of them dag on girls that you have?"

Black said, "Chrissy I'm just so tired of hearing that Christ ain't my son."

Chrissy said, "What?"

Black said, "I have a plan, that one I'll just go on

downtown and have a blood test done."

Chrissy said, "Black you are still going to need his birth certificate. Do you have it, or can you get it. That's one hurdle that you will have to get over in order to prove that you're the father or that you are not listed as the father. Boy all of them girls that you have, you mean to tell me that you don't have no one that works at the social security building?"

Black said," Not as I know of but I might know someone that I can ask though. I'm just so tired of hearing about this dude and that dude that she's been messing with. Lil sis you already know that I'm not even tripping about who she's with, all that I asked of her is to respect me enough and don't have my son's around all of that drama, as long as she'll respect that then it's all good with me, you feel me sis?"

Chrissy said, "Yea I see what you're saying and she'll just have to honor that, because she couldn't ask for anything better than that."

Black said, "The last new thing that I have heard about her was that she was supposed to be messing with the dude Pooh who's supposed to have AIDS."

To be continued.....

Reflections of Baltimore Then

My Memories

Memories
I wouldn't change for anything in the world.

Memories
I will cherish for a lifetime.

The Good Ol'e Dayz

Can't get them back, but glad they are a part of me.

Baltimore Now

ABOUT THE AUTHOR

My name is Christopher White. I'm 37 years old, and I'm from Baltimore, Maryland. When I grew up in a single parent home, mother was battling with substance abuse. This led me to rely on the streets for guidance, not having any positive role models, had caused the start of my adult life to lead me to prison. I thank God for loving me and allowing me this time to get my life right. God has used this setback as a major come back so that He could get the glory through my Urban/Christian Novel's that I have penned.

God has birthed in me a gift to write great books to help our world to see that people can change. These books show my negative actions that have positive results. As an ex-drug dealer, I know it was the Holy Spirit that changed me. My books present a message of how God was working in my life while I was still in my mess. My goal right now is to bring about a spiritual awareness and to build a great spiritual kingdom for those who have experienced the same journey such as I.

You're The Publisher, We're Your Legs

Crystell Publications is not your publisher, but we will help you self-publish your own novel. **We Offer Editing For An Extra Fee, and Highly Suggest It, If Waived, We Print What You Submit!**

Don't have all your money? .... No Problem!
Ask About our Payment Plans
Crystal Perkins-Stell, MHR
Essence Magazine Bestseller
We Give You Books!
PO BOX 8044 / Edmond – OK 73083
www.crystalstell.com
(405) 414-3991

Hey! Stop Wishing and get your book to print NOW!!!

$674.00 Spring POD Special 250 page Manuscript. **Add $75.00** for custom covers.2 Proofs –Publisher & Printer Copy, Mink Magazine Subscription, Free Advertisement, Book Cover, ISBN #, Conversion, Typeset, Correspondence, Masters, 8 hrs Consultation.   *****Inquire about our 100 book plan rates**

$100.00 E-book upload only
$275.00-Book covers/Authors input 1.50
$200.00-Book covers/ templates
$190.00 and up Websites details
$175.00 and up, book trailers

$75 Can't afford edits, Spell-check
$499 Flat Rate Edits Exceeds 210 add
$200-Typeset Book Format PDF File
$200 and up / Type Manuscript Call for
$1.60 Per Page to Type

We're Changing The Game.
No more paying Vanity Presses $8 to $10 per book! We Give You Books @ Cost.

_____ **$7.25 "A Taste of Urban Soup for the People's Soul"**
Order via email: Urbansoup2020@gmail.com